# NEVER SAY NEVER

## ANOTHER ROMANTIC COMEDY WITH ATTITUDE

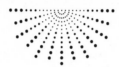

## DONNA MCDONALD

WWW.DONNAMCDONALDAUTHOR.COM

Cover by *MYST Partners*

Edited by *AJ at Blackraven's Designs*

❀ Created with Vellum

# ACKNOWLEDGMENTS

Thanks to my partners in writing crime, J.M. Madden and Robyn Peterman. You keep me honest and make me better at my craft. My writing journey would not be the same without you.

Thanks to AJ for the edit. This was supposed to be an easy one. LOL

Thanks to authors Morgan Malone and Karen Booth, who also write romances with older characters, for reminding me why I chose to do this. You inspired me.

# DEDICATION

*For Mina and her willingness to use her mad photography skills on sexy Silver Fox photos. You rock and I will be looking forward to seeing your vision in photos.*

# ABOUT THIS BOOK

In holidays past, I wrote *Saving Santa*. It was a Christmas story about a wounded female vet. I wrote the story of Megan Lynx, medically retired Marine with a small case of PTSD, for all my female veteran readers and friends. You see many stories about the guys coming home, but not many are about the women who serve. Megan is rough, tough, and what is often called "tomboy". She is also a pure-hearted girl who's been saving her heart for that one guy from her youth that she simply couldn't forget.

In the process of writing Megan's story, I gave her a brother. David Lynx was a guy who stayed at home and went to college while his sister went away. While Megan was serving her country, David was keeping things going back home. David took care of their mother after their father died. David made sure things leveled out. I wrote a Valentine's Day romance, *Kissing Kendra*. It was the story of David finally settling down with a love of his own.

Fast forward to this new series, of which this is Book 2, and I am writing the story of Ann Lynx. Ann is the 50+ year old mother of Megan and David. She's lost a husband, been a single parent, and lived a decade without any consolation. Ann has nearly given up on love completely.

Thinking about that, I decided that Ann needed to be part of *The Perfect Date* series. After seeing her children settled down, the tired mother deserved to have her own story, as all mothers do. So in *Never Say Never*, Book 2 of The Perfect Date series, I have given Ann Lynx her own happily ever after.

I hope you enjoy Ann's story and sexy Cal.

*Happy reading!*
*~ Donna McDonald*

# THE PERFECT DATE SERIES

The essence of all romantic comedy is that falling in love and navigating an unexpected romance is never easy or simple. Instead, it's messy and emotional, and if you're lucky, it's also sexy and fun.

Some relationship professionals, like my character of Dr. Mariah Bates in this series, sincerely want to help people find their perfect love match. For the feisty heroines I've created, many of whom are older, Mariah's going to need all the help she can get.

Or maybe she just needs to step out of the way. You can be the judge.

NOTE ABOUT THE HEAT LEVEL: Not being a fan of the word "clean" when applied to romance, I will instead say the heat level in this new series is in the 1-2 range, rather than 3-4 like some of my others. The focus is on sensuality and I've packed a lot into these stories.

# BOOK DESCRIPTION

*Dating's one thing, but what's love got to do with it?*

Nothing. At least not for Ann Lynx. She's fifty-three for goodness sake. She's had love. All she's in the market for these days is some fun companionship—no strings attached.

Right? Wrong.

Thanks to her pain-in-the-rear-end best friend, Georgia, she's now back on the dating scene. Add Georgia's matchmaking daughter Mariah to the mix and Ann is officially in a world of trouble—or dates—to be more accurate.

All that would be kind of doable, but her handyman's sexy too-young-for-her son is making her feel like a silly young girl. She should definitely stick to the handsome, successful, and older men that Mariah keeps throwing in her path, but she can't seem to banish the sexy Cal from her thoughts anymore than from her broken pantry.

The retired military man is very good at fixing things, and at kissing her senseless. Who's going to fix her though if Cal ends up breaking her heart?

What's love got to do with it? Maybe everything.

# CHAPTER ONE

ANN WAS PULLING ON HER SWEATER WHEN THE DOORBELL RANG. STAN was running late this morning and that meant she was now running late as well. Lateness only mattered because she was stopping by and dragging Georgia Bates along for her trip through makeover purgatory, which apparently was required before dating Mariah's rich, picky clients.

Looking through the security portal in her front door, Ann saw a set of wide shoulders and a bowed head. It wasn't Stan.

A little further down there was a tool belt settled around trim hips. Judging from the beginnings of silver streaks in his hair, she'd put the man's age somewhere in his forties. The tool belt settled on his trim hips told her the most important thing. Though he wasn't Stan, he had likely been sent by him. She'd lost so much time she had no more room to be unsettled.

"Good morning," she said cheerfully, opening the door to find a blue-eyed gaze taking her appearance in with surprise as well.

"Good morning. Your son, David, asked me to come take a look at your broken pantry shelves."

"Sure. Sorry if I seem confused. I was expecting Stan Rodgers."

"Dad wasn't feeling so great today. My name is Cal. I'm Stan's son."

"Cal?" Ann repeated, inviting inside with a sweep of her arm. There was something about the way he was built—the way he carried himself. "Oh, *Calvin*. Now I remember. You're his oldest. Didn't Stan tell me you were in the military?"

"Yes, ma'am. Command Sergeant Major in the Army until about two years ago when I retired. Mom got tired of me moping around. She suggested I come back home and help dad until I made up my mind about what to do with myself. I used to work with him every summer during high school. So here I am wearing a tool belt again. I guess it's true what they say about life coming around full circle as you get older."

"Thank you for your military service, Cal. Glad to see you're still in one piece. A sniper with a bullet retired my Marine daughter early. Glad that didn't happen to you," Ann said, leading the way down the hall to the kitchen.

"Thank you. You should probably know that I've been working part-time for David and helped out during the Christmas parade. Your daughter's a crack shot and that's no lie. I was one of Santa's elves. I helped chase the sniper down. All that running was a pretty hefty workout for an old geezer like me."

Ann nodded, remembering that time. "Nicholas is like my own son. He and David were college roommates and are still the best of friends. My daughter, Megan, loved that boy for years before they ever married. Thank you for whatever part you played in helping save him."

Then what he'd said about himself hit her. Ann fisted a hand on her hip and gave him a chastising look. For pity's sake, anyone could still see his toned chest muscles pushing against the tight t-shirt he wore. Was the man fishing for a compliment or something?

"*Geezer?* What in the world are you talking about? You're still in great shape for someone who's been out of the military for a couple of years."

Eyes crinkled at the corners and Cal laughed at her answer

instead of really responding. Ann let her gaze roam the back of him—which looked equally as impressive in his snug jeans—while a grinning Cal stepped into her walk-in pantry. He eyed the broken shelf with disdain and passed that same judgment on the rest of the space.

"I'll fix the one shelf if that's all you want me to fix, but honestly? I'd replace all these old wooden shelves with wire racks. They're made pretty sturdy these days. Debris falls through and you can just sweep it up from the floor. You can also vary the sizes to make the best use of your storage space."

Ann stepped inside the tiny room with him to better look around. Her wandering gaze wanted to stay on his very nice body every time it landed on him, especially when she found him looking back at her. That kind of interest certainly hadn't happened to her in a while.

However, lustfully ogling the son of her long time handyman seemed a bit sleazy for this early in the morning.

When Cal's back was turned to her again, Ann firmed her mouth. "All that shelf replacing sounds expensive," she said.

"It could be," Cal agreed. "But including my labor, I'm thinking we can get by with a couple hundred dollar version. That's all you need for boxes of cereal and bottles of olive oil. Looks like you only store food in here."

"Because the shelves could never hold any more than that," Ann explained, tipping her head up to look at him.

Now that she was standing so close, she realized Cal had to be at least six feet tall. She suddenly felt tiny and had some trouble breathing around all the male pheromones he was oozing. Needing some fresh air, Ann slipped out into the kitchen again.

"If I take your suggestion, how long will it take to replace all the shelves?"

"Not long." Cal said, looking around again. "Especially not if you empty them for me while I'm out buying the new ones."

Ann shook her head. "I'd normally do it in a heartbeat, but I

3

have an appointment that's going to last all day. I should have already left for it. Want to reschedule?"

"Not particularly. I've got other jobs to do that span the next couple of weeks. Dad was a bit backed up in his work when he got sick." Cal shrugged as he came out of the pantry. "I could probably do everything in one day, even if I have to do the moving. Can I have access to the house while you're gone for your appointment?"

"You're not planning to rob me blind, are you?"

Cal's deep throated laughter was rough and very masculine. His obvious enjoyment of her snarky reply made her smile back at him.

"Sorry. I really didn't mean that. If you ever did anything bad to me, I'd send my children after you. They're both proficient shots."

One of Cal's eyebrows lifted at the threat. His mouth quirked at one corner. "That sort of surprises me. You look like someone who knows how to take care of herself. Will you be home for dinner?"

"I'm not sure, honey. I suggest you don't wait up," Ann teased back, fighting a grin. She crossed her arms, trying to feel as tough as she hoped she sounded. "Are you flirting with me, Cal?"

"No. If I did that, your children wouldn't get a chance to use their weapons. My dad would skin me alive first," Cal said, grinning.

"Really?" Ann asked, surprised a bit because lots of women would be flirting right back with someone who looked like Cal. Wasn't that what she'd been doing? She shook her head. "That's too bad. You were about to make my day. Let me get you a key."

"Yes, ma'am. I'll be right here waiting for you."

Not sure what that meant, Ann wandered off to retrieve the spare she kept hidden in the hallway console table. Returning, she pressed it into the large masculine palm Cal held out to her.

"Just in case I change my mind about the flirting... is it Mrs. or Miss?" he asked.

"It's just Ann," she answered, unsure about why she'd said it quite that way.

"That's a very nice name," Cal said. "Don't worry about a thing. I've got this covered. And I'm sure I'll see you again today."

"And I'm sure I'll be back before you finish my pantry. See you later, Cal."

"Have a good day, Ann."

# CHAPTER TWO

"MY DAUGHTER HAS MORE MONEY THAN BRAINS. I SHOULD HAVE known this was going to be one of those fancy places where they have to get you drunk before they work on you. The problem is that their booze is cheap and your buzz always wears off by the time you have to pay their too expensive bill."

Chuckling over her friend's complaining, Ann turned around on the sidewalk and grabbed the arm of the woman who'd gotten her into this craziness. "Don't even think about trying to run, Georgia Bates. I'm a decade younger and in better shape at the moment because you keep skipping yoga class. You promised to do this stupid makeover with me if I agreed, and you are keeping your word."

"But you know what an extremist my child is. She's not like your two. If my daughter gets her way, I'll have three more colors of hair when they get done. I already have three shades of silver. I don't need total rainbow hair with an expensive dye job I have to upkeep."

Anne grunted and held tight. "It's called highlighting and lowlighting... and it will improve your complexion. And you really, really need that haircut of yours updated. Now don't be such a big baby."

Georgia, who considered herself strong, tried to pull her arm away, but Ann Lynx had a grip of steel. "I can't believe you're so strong. No wonder your daughter joined the Marines. She must be a hoss if she takes after you."

"Lift weights and you can be like me too," Ann ordered, tugging on the arm she held.

Georgia huffed before answering. "You're just tormenting me because you don't want to do this."

Not letting go because she knew better, Ann fisted her free hand on a trim hip kept that way by exercise and not being afraid of hard work. She glared for good measure.

"Gee, you think? *'Come over for a potluck. I'm throwing a food party.'* You tricked me into this, you big old fibber."

Humor kicking in finally—mostly because of Ann's sarcasm—Georgia scrubbed a hand over her face as she laughed. "I'm sorry. It seemed like a good idea at the time. I figured it would be a lark we'd have a good laugh over."

"A lark, sure, but one I have no choice about now because my kids are ecstatic about me doing this. But don't worry, I fully intend to have the last good laugh," Ann said firmly, opening the door and shoving Georgia inside the posh interior. "I'm coming back to watch when Trudy Baxter has to deal with this makeover crap. She vowed never to put on makeup again."

Sighing because they'd been spotted immediately, Georgia plastered a smile on her face for the attendant who took their names and marshaled them into two stylist chairs. Within the hour, they were completely foiled and sitting under dryers. Both were getting manicures and pedicures when Mariah finally came through the door and clapped her hands.

"Yay, you're here. And I see things are moving along fast. Excellent."

"Yay, we're both here..." both women said dryly, making each other laugh.

Mariah rolled her eyes. "Stop whining, you two. You're going to love the results. Manicure. Pedicure. Facial. Makeup. A new hairstyle. You two are getting the works. The image consultant will pick you up here, then it's back to the office for your interviews. I left Della practically vibrating at the thought of making your videos this afternoon."

"Why do I have to make a video? I'm not a real client," Georgia said in the flattest tone she could manage with Ann laughing from the chair beside her.

"You need to go through the whole process with Anne so Trudy won't be able to make you do it. Ann's going to give you a lot less grief. Right, Ann?"

Ann's open snickering earned her the evil eye from Georgia and a grin from Georgia's very clever daughter. She wasn't sure why Mariah was using her to get Georgia to do this, but it was a lot of fun to see her friend squirming.

"Yes. I only wanted some company to lessen the misery. Trudy would put Georgia in stilettos and a miniskirt to get even."

"Like hell," Georgia declared, rolling her eyes when the other female patrons giggled about her loud swearing.

Mariah smiled widely. "It's okay, Mom. Della and I will make the whole process today as painless as possible. Except for the eyebrow tweezing... that always hurts."

The entire salon went silent when a tall, silver-haired man in a suit came through the door. Ann noticed he walked directly to Mariah whose smile grew with every step he took toward her. His one dimple appeared just before he glanced at Georgia and grinned.

"Hey, Handsome," Mariah said, reaching out a hand to pat his chest.

John put a hand on her arm and kissed her cheek. "Been to the bank this morning. The house will be mine in two weeks, just before I go back to work. Still have a few routine inspections that need to be done to satisfy real estate laws."

Mariah bit her lip. "Guess you want an answer from me then, don't you?"

John glanced around. "We can talk later. I just wanted you to know things were going well."

Mariah smiled and rubbed a hand over his arm. "Good. That makes me happy. Need help moving out of your apartment?"

Huffing out a breath, John ran a hand through his hair. "Uh… about that place. It's not really mine. I just have to use it occasionally."

"I see," Mariah said, patting his arm. "Well, that makes me happy too. That place was seriously a bachelor pad."

"Great bed though, huh?" His grin was wicked as he waited for her reply.

Mariah laughed and nodded.

"Okay. So I've got to run a few more errands. Will I see you later?" John asked.

"Absolutely." Mariah went up on her toes, meeting John's lips as they came down to hers. It was a chaste kiss, but his possessive gaze never strayed from hers. The hungry look he gave her before leaving had all the women in the salon fanning themselves.

Grinning over the unexpected show, Ann reached over and poked a gawking Georgia's arm. Her friend luckily turned her way in time to catch her wink. She knew Georgia was nearly wilting in relief over her daughter's new, and promising, relationship. She would feel exactly the same if either of her adult children had gone through what Mariah just had with her cheating ex-husband.

"The man has a nice butt. Bet it looks extra good in jeans," Ann whispered, gleefully giggling when Georgia rolled her eyes. What was wrong with her today? First, she was flirting with her handyman's son. Now she was making dirty jokes.

"Hey now, Ann Lynx. That's my nice butt to stare at. Keep your eyeballs to yourself," Mariah said firmly, narrowing her gaze on the two smirking older women. "I'll find you a guy of your own to ogle soon."

Giggling once more, Ann rubbed her face, which now hurt

from smiling. "I didn't see your name tattooed on the man anywhere, Dr. Bates. Did you, Georgia?"

"I have no idea what you're yammering about," Georgia denied—lying for all she was worth. "But if you think John looks good, wait until you see Hollywood. The guy is your age and dates twenty year olds. Loaded too. He's a real looker if you can get past the 'I'm a bad little boy' thing he's perfected."

Mariah turned her narrowed gaze to her mother. "Are you talking about Dr. Colombo?"

"Some Doctor," she said sarcastically, looking directly at Ann. "Man's dumb as a box of rocks."

"*Mother*," Mariah exclaimed. "Brent is far from dumb. He's a brilliant plastic surgeon—top of his field actually."

Ann felt her freshly plucked eyebrows shoot straight up when Georgia snorted and waved that impressive factoid away with a hand now sporting brightly painted red nails.

"Big deal. That just means Hollywood *makes* those plastic females he dates. It's like he's a grown man playing with dolls. Give me a break, Mariah."

"That's a bit harsh," Ann observed, meaning it as she stared at her angry friend. Why was Georgia so angry over what some random client of Mariah's did for a living? Normally, the woman wouldn't give a good flip. "Why are you being so mean?"

"Mom likes him even though she doesn't want to," Mariah answered for her mother. "And from what Della told me, Dr. Colombo was extremely interested in Mom."

Georgia snorted as she looked away. "Hollywood was not interested in me. He was just being pushy and annoying. He's as pretentious as his watch that cost more than my damn car. So no, I do not like him. He's not my type of man at all."

Ann saw Mariah nod vigorously when her mother wasn't looking. She also mouthed 'really likes him', which had her laughing behind Georgia's stiff back. But it also had her giving her friend a more considering look.

Georgia didn't date either. Trudy and Jellica both had

commented that the lack of a love life was changing Georgia's personality as time went on. Her friend might benefit from having a properly interested man who wanted to soften those sharp edges. Georgia Bates was all hard shell on the outside, but inside she was a marshmallow.

"Take a taxi to the office when you're done with the image consultant. Della will meet you both downstairs with the fare," Mariah ordered. "I have clients this afternoon, but Della will take good care of you."

"That would be a miracle since Della's not even thirty yet. She can barely take care of herself," Georgia declared dryly.

Ann smiled warmly at Georgia's now frowning daughter. It was obvious Georgia was treading on thin ice with such mean teasing. "We'll be there," she promised, trying to soothe the ruffled feelings.

She hoped Mariah would show her a picture of the guy Georgia was complaining about. It would be very interesting to get a look at the first male she'd ever seen make a dent in the emotional armor Georgia never took off. It made her wonder what kind of man could dent hers.

# CHAPTER THREE

"Hi. My name is Ann Lynx and I'm fifty-three years old. I have a Bachelor's Degree in Sociology which I've never used for any job. At the moment, I'm a semi-retired Medical Assistant who still does a little contract work when she wants. My hobbies are reading the classics, visiting with friends, and working out. I do yoga every day because I plan to be in great shape when I'm ninety."

Della smiled softly when she looked up from the camera's display. "Now tell us something unique about yourself— something only your closest, most trusted friends know about you."

Ann laughed nervously. "Okay. You might want to pause while I think about that for a minute. I'm not that interesting a person."

Her shiny red lips felt like they were covered in six layers of goo as she smiled and she wanted to rub five of them off. The feeling was highly distracting. Della and Mariah had both approved the heavy makeup that had taken an hour for the esthetician to apply.

"Let me see. Something no one knows about me..."

Georgia cleared her throat discreetly and stepped away from the wall. She was standing behind Della and... *what in the world was the crazy woman doing now?* Georgia's body leaned one way and then another. Luckily the blue dress with matching blue heels gave with each of her jerky movements. She stopped and glared directly at Ann, rolled her eyes, and then mimed doing a ballet pose.

*Dancing!* Oh yes. God… Georgia was dancing. Or trying to.

Laughing loudly at her slowness in figuring it out, Ann's embarrassed smile finally appeared for the camera. "I belly dance. Well, actually… I used to teach belly dancing. It's a great form of exercise. I never did it professionally, but my husband used to love it when I danced for him."

Her face fell as she winced. Wow. That came out without any filtering. She'd forgotten that she wasn't talking to her friends.

"Sorry. I've been a widow for a very long time and haven't dated in a while. I guess it's poor form to mention other men during your dating video, right?"

Della grinned as she shrugged. "Honesty is always good. I'll edit your answers… or ask for a retake if I need to. Don't worry about it."

Ann nodded and made herself relax again. She looked beyond Della and saw Georgia leaning against the wall once more, this time doing her best and most serene Grace Kelly impersonation.

Her friend was mercurial and intense and even a little bit unhinged at times. Why was Mariah so calm and logical? She must have taken after her father—someone Ann had never met. She'd befriended Georgia Bates during a group grief counseling session for widows.

"Tell us a little about your perfect match, Ann. What's he look like? What does he do for a living?"

"Are you serious?" Ann asked.

Della nodded, grinning the whole time.

Ann bit her lip, then hoped she hadn't gotten lipstick on her teeth. No more smiling now, she decided. She hummed a bit as she thought. An image of a grinning Calvin Rodgers and his wide shoulders leapt into her mind. Maybe she did need to take this seriously. A long denied itch for sex was making a reappearance. Maybe she needed to find someone appropriate to scratch it.

"I've never stopped to consider what my perfect match would look like. Liking the way someone looks is so subjective. No sane woman would ever kick a man she considered handsome out of her bed... I mean... out of her life. If I have to make a list, it would be more about who he is as a person. The perfect man would be funny with me, charming to strangers, and willing to help do the dishes after dinner. Those traits may not seem glamorous by today's standards, but I know from experience they're a gift in a real relationship."

When Ann ran down, Della smiled at her. "Anything else you want to add?"

Ann took a deep breath. This was a chance to say the one thing she'd never had with any man she'd ever dated. This was probably her last and only chance to ask for what she'd like. She drew in another breath, smiling at the camera first.

"I think it would be nice to date someone who loved his work with a sincere passion. Life is far too short not to do work you absolutely love. I think being happy with how you're making a living automatically makes you a confident, happy, and very interesting person to spend time with. Is that okay to say?"

"Yes. Anything is okay. I noticed you're fairly tall for a woman. Can your perfect man be shorter than you?" Della asked.

Ann laughed at the question, because behind Della, Georgia was rolling her eyes and then her whole head. Georgia and Trudy were tall too. Jellica was the only shorty in their group and the only one who got asked out on a regular basis. They'd often talked about their non-existent dating lives and laughed at the shortage of men taller than the three of them. Though she was not a big fan of them, this situation merited a white lie or at least a slightly varnished truth.

"I've never thought about height really, but I would like a man who thought looking good for me was important. It would be hard for me to respect someone who didn't care as much as I did about how he looked."

"That's totally understandable. Any last words?" Della prompted.

Ann let a relieved sigh escape. "It's very strange to record yourself and your opinions in a video. I'm not sure how much of who I am will be shown through this recording. Nothing really substitutes for meeting face-to-face, does it? I guess that's an old school dating sort of attitude."

Della finally stopped the recording. "It's very reasonable. You're going to find most of the men you'll meet will feel the same way you do. Most become clients because they're tired of bar hopping and online dating sites where practically no one tells the truth. Mariah's average for finding quality dates for people is very high. She has a real gift for matching up people who have genuine things in common."

Ann nodded as she stood. "Will I get to see the video before it becomes available?"

"If you like," Della said with a sly smile, "but we're going to have to use it until we can do a second one, even if you hate it. The real purpose of the video is to show what you look like and share a bit of your personality. You came across great and not wooden at all, Ann."

Della tapped on her keyboard and then looked behind her. "Okay. You're up next, Georgia. Have a seat."

Sighing in resignation, Georgia walked around a grinning Della. Ann giggled and pinched Georgia on the arm as she passed, making her friend swear at her.

Georgia took the recording hot seat, crossing her glossed bare legs at the ankles to keep herself from bolting. Her chin lifted at a smirking Della busily adjusting the camera angle. She probably didn't want to crop off the three hundred dollar hairstyle Mariah had paid for that morning.

"Okay, Georgia. Start with your name and tell us a bit about yourself," Della ordered.

"I'm Georgia Bates. I'm sixty years old and can't believe I let my daughter talk me into making this stupid video. Don't get me wrong—Mariah is a brilliant woman and does excellent work for her clients. However, like every other adult child left with a single living parent, she likes to meddle in her mother's life—*in my life*— under the pretense of getting me to *take more chances*," Georgia finished dryly, making quote marks in the air with her red painted fingernails. "Frankly, I like my life as it is. I like myself. I do what I want, when I want, and I don't intend to stop. THAT's my idea of being happy."

Della bit the inside of her cheek to keep from laughing. "So you're not really interested in finding your perfect match? Or in dating?"

Georgia frowned and glanced off. "I didn't say that... not exactly." She dug for honesty and found a little. "It's just that I've become picky about men as I've gotten older. I can't afford to play stupid games anymore. If I found someone that interested me as a man AND as a person, then of course I'd date him, or at least sleep with him. You're not meant to marry every person you feel a passing fancy about. I've seen too many widowed and divorced friends make the mistake of marrying the first person they boi..."

Ann's indrawn breath was followed by a coughing fit of shock that she pretended to fight. Georgia's glare at being interrupted had her biting her fist to stop all noise making. But where were Georgia's filters? Didn't she have any?

"As I was saying..." Georgia continued, forcing herself to smile as she stared into the damn camera. "I don't have time for games. No ego stroking. No mothering a man who can't take care of himself. There's only one reason to date someone. You date them because they're interesting, fun, and they get your engine revving. I don't see any reason not to just say that plainly. Not that I recommend casual bed hopping—because I don't—but I do recommend cutting through the crap of trying to be something you're not. That kind of thing always comes out in a relationship. Am I right, Dr. Livingston?"

Della nodded. "You are exactly right, Georgia." She paused then grinned. "What's your perfect man like?"

Georgia snorted. "There's no such thing as a perfect man... or a perfect woman. There's just two flawed people trying to get to know each other and that should be good enough. Flaws make a person interesting. I do find it hard to respect a man who doesn't know what a freaking water shut off is under a toilet. Why would you ever cook dinner for someone like that? Personally, I have better things to do with my time."

Della burst out laughing and pressed the stop button. "Okay. I think we're done. Or at least I am. Both your interviews were wonderfully refreshing."

"Great," Georgia said, hearing the sarcasm tucked into the praise. "Is the torture really over now? All this nonsense has made me have to use the bathroom."

Ann glared at her friend when Della covered her mouth to stifle more laughter.

"Honestly, Georgia. Would it kill you to at least try to be a good sport? You answered like the worst she-woman man hater in the world," she chastised, only to start giggling uncontrollably at the blank look of confusion she got in response.

# CHAPTER FOUR

A̲n̲n̲ ̲s̲a̲w̲ ̲S̲t̲a̲n̲'s̲ ̲t̲r̲u̲c̲k̲ ̲s̲t̲i̲l̲l̲ ̲p̲a̲r̲k̲e̲d̲ ̲i̲n̲ ̲h̲e̲r̲ ̲d̲r̲i̲v̲e̲w̲a̲y̲ ̲w̲h̲e̲n̲ ̲s̲h̲e̲ got home, which meant his handsome son was still at her house. She pulled her Civic into the garage and climbed out.

She told herself the only reason she hadn't changed back into her normal clothes was a lack of time. But that wasn't really the reason. The man in her pantry was. She was kind of curious to see if Cal would flirt with her again when he saw her like this.

The tiny beige kitten heels showing off the length of her full-skirted green dress made click clack sounds as she walked across the cement garage and through her tiled laundry room. The dress hit a good three inches above her knees in a length she never would have chosen alone. The image consultant Mariah worked with had insisted it suited her personality and style.

"Great timing, Ann. I just finished..." Cal's gruff voice drifted off as he stopped and stared... and stared some more.

Ann felt her face heat under his gaze. Even her husband had never looked at her in quite that way. Cal must not be dating anyone. Otherwise, he wouldn't be acting so... deprived. His appreciative whistle had the red creeping up and down until embarrassment covered her.

"Wow. Whatever you did today, it was worth every penny it cost. You look fantastic. Nice legs... I mean, dress."

"Thank you," Ann said politely, reaching up to nervously play with the gold butterfly charm necklace she'd worn that morning. It was the only item Della had let her keep on. "I had a complete makeover. It's part of a project I'm working on with some of my older friends. I had to make a video today."

Cal blinked a few times, but continued to stare. "I'm sure you looked great on camera."

Ann shrugged, more pleased by his comments than she was willing to admit... or show. "Pantry work finished?" she asked.

Cal nodded slowly, still dazed. "Yes, I was just putting things away. I took a few liberties with your organization. I hope you don't mind."

When he turned to walk back into the tiny space, Ann bit her bottom lip. When was the last time she'd felt so female? It had been... well, it had been ages. Maybe that was why she felt so strange around Cal.

Following him into the tiny room, Ann smiled at the new shelving with all her pantry items now neatly on display. True to his word, Cal had given her all kinds of storage. He'd even created a space big enough for the extra appliances she'd been storing on top of her refrigerator. They now sat in a tidy bottom row waiting to be needed.

"This is great—really great," Ann declared, reaching out to touch the wire racks. They did feel substantial, just like he promised they would. "Wonderful work, Cal. I'm glad I said yes to you."

She turned to see him silently staring. His intense perusal made her a bit nervous, so she did what she always did in tense situations. She laughed nervously and got sarcastic. "You're staring like you've never seen a woman in makeup before." Cal gave a man grunt that had her ducking her head in embarrassment for being so bold with him.

"Been a while since I've seen one who looked quite as good as you do at the moment. I thought you looked cute this morning…"

"*Cute?*" Ann repeated, laughing at his words. Could a woman over fifty still be cute? Wasn't there an age limit on that kind of description?

"… but your new look is a magical transformation," Cal declared, pausing to look her up and down. "I'm wishing like hell I had on my dress uniform so I could ask you out to dinner. A woman who looks as good as you do right now needs to go out and be shown off."

Ann swallowed with difficulty because there was now an emotional lump in her throat. How did Cal keep throwing her so off balance? "If I'm not responding glibly enough, it's because I'm not used to hearing so many compliments in a single day. You exceeded my limit in the last ten minutes."

Cal chuckled, then grinned at her. He reached out, took her hand, and lifted her knuckles to his lips. The feel of his warm mouth against her skin sent a shiver down her spine.

He kept his gaze on her knuckles as he spoke. "I haven't felt like dating much in the last couple of years, so I'm out of practice. Do you think we could maybe have dinner for real sometime?"

Ann opened her mouth to tell him they couldn't do that, but the refusal refused to come out of her mouth. What did finally emerge was shocking.

"Are you in a hurry to get home this evening? I can offer you some leftover beef stew with spicy cornbread. One of my friends is a retired chef and she taught me the recipe. It's really good as long as you eat it hot."

Cal grinned, rubbing a thumb over her knuckles. He squeezed her hand tighter as he answered. "Just so I know I'm not imagining this… you want me to stay tonight?"

"For dinner, Cal. That's all I'm offering," Ann said softly. "I just…"

Cal chuckled, squeezed her hand again, and then quickly

released it. "I'd love to eat with you. Let me just put the rest of the pantry stuff away."

Ann nodded. She looked down at herself. "Do you mind if I change out of this outfit?"

Grinning, Cal shook his head. "Are you kidding? I can't wait to see what you pick to wear next. It's been fun watching you change clothes all day."

"I usually just wear my yoga clothes around the house." His masculine groan set her face on fire. She swallowed her nervousness and spoke the rest of her thoughts. "And I swear I don't make a habit of inviting strange men to hang around for meals."

"Glad to hear I'm your exception," Cal said. "And I won't tell my father about this, if you won't."

His teasing about Stan made her giggle. "How old are you, Cal? Seventeen?"

"Yes... times two and a half."

Ann studied the ceiling for a moment trying to do the math in her head. Cal's laughter had her looking back at him.

"I'm forty-three," he supplied. "I've been divorced over a decade and have two daughters. One is in college. The other graduates high school in a year."

Ann nodded, smiling softly in sympathy. "Divorce can be hard. My friend's daughter just went through a nasty one. It's hard on the whole family."

Cal nodded and then shrugged. "Like most military men, I was gone a lot. Not every woman can handle that kind of life. My ex discovered she couldn't. We divorced and I never remarried, not even after she did. What's most important is that the girls and I are fine. Their stepfather is a decent guy. They live outside of Dayton, and when we're together, we all get along. Things could be much, much worse than I have it."

Ann nodded in agreement. "I've always counted my blessings that my marriage was as strong as it was. Can you believe that I've never lived anywhere else in my life but Norwood? The Cincinnati area is all I know. And I'm fifty-three."

"You're over fifty? Wow, you're my first older woman," Cal teased.

"I'm not actually your anything," Ann replied haughtily, but the effect was spoiled by the corner of her mouth twitching.

Cal grinned at her and dropped his gaze to her legs. When it lifted, the look in his eyes made every nerve ending flutter inside her.

"*Yet*, Ann... you're not my anything *yet*. Isn't that such a great word?"

Cal then made a shooing motion at her with his hands. The action sent her into giggles as she backed out of the pantry to let him pass by her.

"I don't mean to be rude, but I have to finish this job. I've got a hot date tonight with a woman in yoga clothes. I don't want to keep her waiting too long."

∼

ANN FILLED CAL'S BOWL A SECOND TIME, THEN BROUGHT THE REST OF the pan to the table. The way he was eating, she knew he'd be able to finish it all. She set the remaining stew close to him, pushing the pan with the remainder of Trudy's special cornbread closer as well.

Fetching two more beers from the refrigerator, she set one by his plate and opened the other for herself. Some liked their wine—and she liked a glass now and again—but she loved imported beer and always kept a cold six pack on hand. It was a special treat for her.

Ann brought one leg up into her chair and curved her arm around her knee. This was her favorite way to sit. It made her feel like things were normal despite her sexy, masculine, and very distracting company.

"Finish the rest of the stew if you can. I've had all I want of it and the rest will just get tossed later," she told him.

Nodding absently, Cal watched every move she made as she wiggled and got more comfortable. He was eating the whole time he stared at her. The man looked the way she imagined a hungry wolf would look plowing through his first meal after nearly starving. Didn't anyone ever feed him?

"You keep staring at me, Cal. I know I scrubbed those six layers of red lipstick off before I started cooking."

"That's not it," he said.

Ann giggled. "Never seen a woman drink two beers before?" She knew her sass had gotten her into trouble again when his eyes narrowed.

"I've never seen a woman drink two beers who looks as good as you do. Unless you're wearing one of those all over make-me-look-skinny things under your clothes. Are you?"

Ann rolled her eyes. "That was not a polite question, you know."

Cal guiltily moved his stare to the remainder of his stew. "I guess now you know why I'm still single after all this time."

Ann snickered over his social discomfort and took another drink of her beer. She hadn't meant to make him feel bad.

"If you must know... I'm not wearing anything at all under my clothes. I work out for the sole purpose of being about to eat and drink anything I want. You have to do that at my age when you have friends who cook better than you do. God save me from anyone who hates carbs. I hate those people, don't you?"

Cal's spoon clattered to his bowl as it fell, and she laughed at his flinching over it.

"What's wrong now?" she asked, pretending to be exasperated.

"Sorry. I'm a guy. All I heard was the nothing-under-your-clothes part of your speech."

She laughed harder when Cal lifted his already opened beer and drank the remaining one-third of it before stopping.

"I'm sorry if I've embarrassed you with my frankness," Ann said, not really meaning the apology... and she figured they both knew it.

The truth was she was enjoying the masculine attention Cal was showing her. It had been a very long time since she'd had male company across her dinner table. Not even David ate with her very often. Her son was too busy running his business. Her daughter, Megan, hovered and worried when she came by. Children could never really replace the company of a spouse. On some level, Ann supposed her children finally understood that after finding their own life partners.

Cal shook his head as he sipped from the fresh beer. "I'm not embarrassed at all—not by anything you say. I just feel like I've been hit by a train I didn't see coming. Today has been very surprising for me."

Ann laughed. "What in the world does that mean?"

"I like you, Ann… and I'd like…" he paused, looking guilty again. "I'd like to like you even more if you'd let me."

Giggling, Ann felt her face flame at his poor innuendo. "Are you trying to say you'd like to sleep with me without actually saying it?"

Cal widened his eyes and took a big bite of cold cornbread to keep from replying.

"It's okay, Cal. You're my first bold move in about thirty years. I feel the tug between us too, but I don't do that sort of thing, not even with random, handsome men I invite to dinner in a moment of weakness."

Cal nodded. "You know… I'm both relieved and disappointed. Never felt that combination before. It's an interesting feeling. Yet also somehow appropriate. Strange."

Ann smiled at his candid reaction. "I think it's just been this day. My friend's daughter runs this very expensive dating service. Somehow I got talked into becoming a client—not a real one, mind you—just enough of one to get my children to quit worrying about me being alone. I've been a widow for close to a decade now and haven't really dated much. Truthfully? I haven't really wanted to."

Cal swallowed his food, took a drink, and then brought his gaze to hers. "So…" he waved a hand at her, "you got all dolled up

25

today to join a dating service to make David and Megan think you were really dating again?"

Ann sighed and nodded. "Yes. And please don't rat me out to them. I thought I'd hate the whole process. I left this morning intending to hate the makeover part. But the truth is... I didn't hate it. When I came home and you reacted so..."

"Like a normal guy who got blown away when he saw a beautiful woman standing two feet away from him looking like she needed to be kissed?" Cal prompted.

Ann grinned and nodded again. "Yes. What can I say? It's been a very long time. It was nice to feel pretty again. That's why I asked you to stay for dinner. Do you understand?"

Cal nodded. "I do. But you were also pretty this morning before you did anything fancy to yourself. I couldn't stop thinking about you all day. The rest with you all fixed up... it was like a fantasy coming to life. Your new hairstyle is very flattering by the way, but I've never known how to say anything like that to a woman without her cringing."

"Well, I'm not cringing. I'm flattered. It's very sweet of you to tell me, Cal."

Cal frowned. "Not really as sweet as you think. I'm just being honest. Why can't you believe I find you sexy?"

"Oh, I do," Ann said, sighing around her beer. "I just don't know what to do about it. Getting churned up about how I look and caring about you noticing... that's all like trying to get in touch with a part of myself I haven't seen in a while."

"If you don't know what to do with me and my interest, it really has been a long time for you," Cal joked.

Giggling over his smirk, Ann sobered enough to take the last drink of her beer. "I appreciate your company and your flirting. It was a nice pretend date for me. I haven't spent this much time with a man other than my son in literally years. I hope that's another confidence you'll keep."

Cal finished his beer, stood, and carried his dishes to the sink. "Can I help you clean up?"

The woman in her melted a little... and Cal hadn't seen the video she'd made today. He was being considerate, but that didn't make him meant for her. He was much too young and much too ... male. Yes, that was it. Sexual heat rolled off him whenever she got close. Cal was far too male for a woman who'd been without one for such a long time. Today was just a pleasant, unexpected interlude in both their lives.

"There's only a few things to wash, Cal. I can get them. I'm sure you're tired after working all day. You need to get home."

Tearing her gaze from his now sad one, Ann rose from her seat and fetched the check she'd written out to Stan's business earlier. She handed it over after Cal collected the tool belt he'd hung from one of the new racks in the pantry.

She walked him to her front door, opening it to let him leave. Cal stopped and turned to her.

"This has been the best day I've had since I got out of the military. Can I kiss you goodnight?" he asked.

Letting a long nervous breath escape the confines of her tight chest, Ann reluctantly nodded. Cal's lips touched hers slowly, the warmth of his kiss seeping into every cell as his mouth slid confidently across hers. She heard a soulful moan, but wasn't sure which of them made it.

A strong hand slipped around her waist, then fell to her backside. Cal used it to drag her whole body up against the front of his. Their kiss changed instantly from something innocent to something needy and desperate, complete with mutual writhing against each other trying to appease the longing to connect.

It was too wonderful for words. It was also too much too fast.

Using a now trembling hand, Ann gently pushed their bodies apart. She also took a step back. It was the only way she could breathe.

"I don't care about our differences. Will you at least think about giving this attraction we have a chance?" Cal whispered.

Ann closed her eyes, trying to think of an honest reply that wouldn't hurt his feelings. She only opened them when she heard a truck starting. She watched Cal smile and wave before driving away.

Feeling lonely now and not liking it at all, Ann closed the door and tried to forget her strange, strange day.

# CHAPTER FIVE

ANN TURNED OVER THE PHOTOS SLOWLY, SHOCK RENDERING HER MUTE. All the men were handsome. Every one of them. And if Georgia was right... all of them were also very rich... since they were willing to drop some major bucks just to meet potential women.

"I don't understand. Why are there so many?"

Mariah smiled as she leaned back in her chair. "Because every man I showed your profile to now wants to meet you."

Terror had Ann's eyes flying to the smiling doctor's. "You're kidding."

Mariah shook her head. "No. No, I'm not."

Ann slipped one pic out and held it up. She pointed to it. "He looks younger than my son... except for the tats. But his hair— what was he thinking? Do women really like dating guys who look like this? How old is this guy?"

Mariah's twinkling laughter over her comments had Ann narrowing her eyes. She was being serious. Didn't she sound serious?

"That one's not wanting a date anytime soon, but Elliston has become my test case for the whole younger man older woman phenomena. The last woman I fixed him up with was in her early forties. They ended up good friends and now he's going to her wedding."

Even though she hated when Georgia did it, Ann rolled her eyes to the ceiling over the news.

"Young people these days seem to date within groups from what I've seen. My children are the exception. They were quick to bond for life when they fell in love—just like I did. Megan and Nicholas barely got together before they married. David had a wild side for a couple of years, but he met Kendra and moved in with her. It took forever for him to marry her though—that was the only way he was like other guys his age."

Mariah smiled as she rocked her chair. "Elliston is over thirty and busy building his business. He is definitely not interested in marriage. He just wants company occasionally—good, intelligent company. He wants it more than sex, which he says is far too easy to get. I know this because he bluntly told me so."

Ann made a face. "Sorry, but I don't think I could ever handle dating a man that young. It would be like spending time with David and I don't need more children in my life."

Her mind replayed Cal tugging her to him to kiss her... and how hard it had been to sleep after he'd left. "Someone in their forties might be okay. A decade younger is probably my limit."

Mariah nodded. "Noted. It's totally your choice to say no to any of them."

"How can I say anything? I'm overwhelmed. Are you sure all of these men want to date me?" Ann asked again, still trying to accept it.

"Yes. They read your bio, watched your video, then asked for the first meet. What surprises you most about their interest?"

Ann shrugged. "I'm not sure. I know I'm nothing special as a woman. Sure the makeover helped create a temporary illusion, and I admit I looked my best afterward. But Mariah... underneath that glamor you paid for is a woman who married the only man she ever slept with. I'm not exciting enough to merit this kind of attention from men."

"Monogamy in a person is very alluring these days. Plus, I think your description of the perfect match was a challenge to the men who asked to meet you." Mariah pointed at the folder. "Those men are all wondering if they might be the kind of man you talked about. Also, I think it came across that you weren't going to settle. The confidence of a woman knowing what she wants—and doesn't want—resonates with nearly all men of substance."

"Men of substance?" Ann asked.

Laughing, Mariah slowly nodded as her smile grew. "That's my term. Men tend to define their personalities by how successful they are in business. What it means for you is that the men in your match folder are successful, passionate businessmen, just like you requested."

Ann chuckled nervously. "That was off the cuff. Trust me, I did not ask for any of this. Georgia tricked me."

"That fight is between you and my mother. Just remember it's not like you have to pick one and then marry the guy," Mariah explained around a smile. "Most of my clients just want a nice, pleasant dinner date they don't have to worry will get the wrong ideas or create a drama they don't have time to deal with. Sometimes they only want a dance partner for an evening. They have money and spend it on all kinds of things. I rarely have anyone challenge my fees."

Remembering one thing she'd said in her video, a blushed climbed her face. "Oh lord, they all know I belly dance, don't they? I said that in the video. Are they going to expect me to dance for them?"

Mariah giggled as she shrugged. "I'm sure your disclosure drew some interest, but I don't think it will come up on a first date."

Ann put her hands to her hot cheeks. "I'm totally embarrassed now."

"Let's look at this differently. Want to know which guy I have in mind for you?" Mariah asked.

Nodding, Ann shoved the folder full of at least a dozen men

back across the desk. Mariah sorted through them, then passed one photo back. Ann took it and looked at it. The man was very handsome. And he was older.

"Is he my age?" Ann asked.

"Yes. Your age," Mariah said, confirming the guess.

Then she saw the name on the bottom. "Mariah? Isn't this the guy Georgia likes?"

"Yes," Mariah said firmly. "He's also the guy who needs an already trained dancing date for some charity event he's being honored at. Do you do any ballroom dancing?"

"I do all kinds of dancing, but..." Ann paused, chewing on her lip. Nasty habit, but one she couldn't seem to break. "What about Georgia?"

"Mom swears she's not interested and Brent deserves someone nice. You're the nicest woman I know amongst Mom's friends."

"Thank you," Ann said on autopilot. "But I thought this guy always dated younger women."

"No. That was Mom being judgmental. Brent dates all kinds of women and he recently confirmed for me that age isn't an issue," Mariah said, leaning over her desk. "I figure you'll either like him for yourself, or be able to tell me if he's worth what it will take to convince my mother to go out with him."

Her mouth dropped open in shock. "You want me to check him out for Georgia?"

Mariah shrugged, her mouth twisting in sheepish amusement. "Only if you want to be his dance partner for an evening. Brent's a sweetie and a charmingly attentive date, at least at first, from what I hear. However, he has adult children problems and tends to become easily distracted after he gets to know a woman. The reviews on him are mixed, but he truly does look even better in person than in that picture. I'm sure he would be a great man to ease back into dating with. His interest in my mother is not his normal reaction to women. Usually he's more laid back about them."

"Is Georgia right about him being a bad boy?"

"Not in the way she thinks he is," Mariah said, grinning at Ann's surprise. "Brent loves women... sincerely loves women. His career is based on that love. Before his first wife died, she was disfigured in a car accident. He fixed her completely and her successful recovery helped him build his still phenomenal career. She was beautiful right up until she passed away from cancer. Honestly, I don't think he ever got over her."

Ann let out a sad breath. "You said his first wife. Did I hear that right? How many times has he been married?"

Mariah hummed as she thought. "I think four or five times—the latter ones all with prenuptial agreements—the man is super smart about people. He finally stopped marrying after I started fixing him up with the occasional match. Now he just enjoys female company for a while, but it doesn't last. This is why I'm not keen to fix him up with my mother."

"So what is this about me dating him? I don't know, Mariah." Ann studied the handsome man in the photo. "If Georgia does like him, even a little, me dating him could hurt her. I don't want to do that. I like your mother."

"The event Brent needs a dance partner for is nothing intimate—not like a real date. Think of this as him hiring you as a dance instructor for the evening. What you learn about him can help all of us, including Mom. If she's correct about Brent, I need to get her mind off him fast. Right?"

"I suppose that's true," Ann admitted.

Mariah dug through the folder again. She pulled out one more photo and passed it over. "Look at this guy too. His name is Lincoln Walker. He has a hot air balloon and a helicopter tour business. Of all the men in your folder, next to Brent, Lincoln is the most passionate about his work. He just turned fifty and is a two year widower. He's had a few dates, but is still looking for the magic to happen with someone."

Ann studied the man. Looking at him didn't set her nerves singing, but... "He's very handsome too."

"Yes. Like Brent, Lincoln's also one of those guys who's going to stay handsome his entire life. He's tall too. I think you would genuinely like him, Ann. Why don't you go out with him this week? Lincoln's a very laid back kind of person as well. He'd be a great first date for you."

Ann bit her lip again. That's what she'd called Cal. Was dinner with him last night more of a real date than she'd realized? How would she even know after not dating for so many years? Maybe if she went out with just the two Mariah picked from the folder, she could back out of any others without hurting anyone's feelings.

"Lincoln sounds nice enough. What do I need to do?"

Mariah's pleasure and excitement had her leaning over the desk. "There's a coffee shop in your neighborhood. Would you be willing to meet Lincoln there just to say hi and chat for a few minutes? Either of you can cancel after that if there's no interest in setting up a real date. I don't like to charge my clients if we can figure out early there's no chemistry between them worth pursuing."

It sounded like a lot of pre-nothing hullabaloo to go through for coffee, but Ann nodded. She supposed the guy deserved two meetings since he'd be the one paying Mariah's expensive fees.

"I'll text you when Lincoln gets back to me with a time. I'm hoping I can work it out without affecting your yoga class schedule. Mom said you were teaching some of the classes now."

Ann nodded and sighed as she rose. "I'm just a fill in. This is more important at the moment."

Because the sooner she got these next couple of weeks over with, the sooner she could get back to her real life.

# CHAPTER SIX

For once Georgia hadn't skipped yoga class. Instead, she'd cornered Ann in the parking lot after and grilled her about her meeting with Mariah. Ann had told her friend everything about Lincoln the hot air balloon operator, but absolutely nothing about Brentwood Colombo looking for a dance partner.

Feeling guilty for the omission, but not up to dealing with Georgia's potentially hurt feelings, Ann had slunk home in her blue Civic, cursing her own stupidity. Her punishment was that the garage door flatly refused to go down all the way. And now it seemed completely stuck.

She couldn't remember the door ever being replaced. Her husband had installed it when Megan was in middle school. She'd been meaning to replace it the last time it had acted up, but David had done some man magic and gotten it to work again.

After that, she hadn't wanted to spend the money, since the door had continued to work. Luckily the door leading into the house locked, but she really didn't want to risk her garage getting cleaned out by thieves overnight. That left her few options for dealing with this.

She thought about calling a garage door company herself, but knew David would pitch a fit if she didn't talk to him about it first. His take was that the door lifting mechanism just needed batteries again—the former "magic" she'd not understood before—but under no circumstances was she to climb up there herself.

David would either be over later or send help. She was to do nothing but wait until then.

Waiting for Ann meant standing under the mechanical box on the garage ceiling and frowning up at it. She knew Georgia would have been up on a ladder and fixed it already. Why hadn't she developed that kind of skillset and daring? Shouldn't a woman over fifty be more self-sufficient than she was?

Her head turned when she heard a vehicle pull into her driveway. A few moments later the garage door got pushed up despite the broken door. Cal grinned when he saw her standing there, his gaze dropping to her slim-legged yoga crops and sandaled feet with red painted toes on full view. By the time his eyes found their way back to her face, she was heated from his perusal and flushed with the guilt of her dirty thoughts about him.

It didn't help when he reached blindly behind him and pulled the garage door completely back down, closing them inside the now semi-dark room.

"Now why didn't I think of doing that," Ann said, her voice trembling just a bit more than she was comfortable admitting to herself.

"People always forget their garage doors still work manually," Cal said, shrugging a shoulder. "Don't be surprised if you get a call. Dad gave me a strange look when I nearly ran out of the house to get here after David hung up."

Ann closed her eyes. "It wasn't like I broke my garage door on purpose just to see you again."

"This is kismet, then?" Cal suggested.

Ann chuckled at his choice of words, and could see Cal was trying hard not to laugh at her refusal to admit she enjoyed seeing him again.

"No. The correct word is *procrastination*," Ann replied. "I'm sure there are a dozen things around here that should have been repaired or replaced long ago."

Cal spread his arms wide. "Perfect. Everything you break just gives me more excuses to come back."

"Stan should be thrilled with you then. It's also more money for him."

Cal threw the door back up before smiling at her. "Move your car out so I can get under the gearbox. I'll change the batteries for you."

Ann nodded and fetched her keys. Once her car was in the driveway, she walked back inside. "I'm going to be embarrassed if all it needs is batteries. I could have done that myself."

Chuckling, Cal fetched a ladder from where it had hung on the wall. "Safer not to climb unless it's an emergency. I'm going to leave my cell so you can call me for little things like this. I can't charge you for changing batteries."

Ann stared at his body as he climbed. He looked very good to her... very good. Much better than handsome Lincoln's picture, or even the man Georgia thought was good looking.

And she definitely needed to stop ogling his forty-three year old body.

"Of course you can charge me, Cal. It's called a service call. I've paid them many times."

Cal smirked as he undid the cover. "You're so funny. I need two double-As. Got any? That was not a joke about your bra size. I know you're bigger than that."

Ignoring his teasing explanation, Ann nodded and hustled into the house. She returned with the fresh batteries and handed them up. He handed the two bad ones down to her. Fresh batteries now in place, he told her to try the door switch. She hit it and watched as the door rose smoothly with no complaining at all. It also went back down the same.

Cal was refastening the cover when she walked to the ladder and looked up again. "I can't believe David called you out here for batteries. I thought the whole thing was broken."

"And that's why you're so cute. Actually, David had no idea. He called my father who's feeling much better and wanted to come himself," Cal corrected as he climbed down the ladder. "I came because I wanted to see you again. One of us needs to admit the truth here."

"Cal…"

His hand reaching out to push the hair off her face stopped her tongue and her brain.

"This is just a simple man liking woman thing. Don't over think it. Want to grab some dinner with me?" he asked.

Ann looked down at herself. "I'm not really dressed for going out."

"Neither am I," he said. "I was thinking of that salad place by the mall. It has great subs too. No one will care what we look like."

She bit her lip and really looked at him. He was grinning at her with a dare in his eyes. Coffee with a balloon operator didn't hold half as much appeal as eating with Cal tonight.

"Okay, I'll go… but only if you let me pay your Dad a service call fee. God forbid he think I'm going out with you to get out of paying."

"Dad would never…"

Ann held up a hand to stop his denial.

Cal sighed heavily, but finally nodded. "Fine. I'm buying dinner then," he groused.

"Fine. Let me get a sweater. I hate being cold. You never know with restaurants."

"Want me to warm you up? I'll happily do that for free. Dad won't mind. I promise," Cal teased.

"Sweater… and we'll take *my* car. I see your father's truck and dollar signs start dancing in my head."

～

"If you had unlimited money, what would you do?" Ann asked. They'd finished their food, but were still sipping their drinks and talking. Cal was very pleasant company when he wasn't flirting so hard.

His shrug took a lot of time to manifest. "I thought about going to school. I've never done that, except for military training. I have no idea what I'd go for though, which is why I haven't signed up. The Army is all I've known, but I have zero interest in anything remotely related to tanks, guns, or artillery of any sort. I want something new... something to spark my passion."

"Like what?" Ann asked. "What do you like to do?"

Cal looked around. "I think it would be fun to be an investor. I like finance. I like economics. I'm just not sure how a person can make money doing it."

"You can definitely make money," Ann said with confidence, because she had. "I took an investing class and bought Amazon stock when it was less than three dollars a share. That's worked out quite well for me. The money I've made investing nicely supplements my retirement. I still work part-time, but I don't actually have to work at all, so long as I live frugally. The house got paid off when my husband died. I'm a lucky woman."

Cal grinned. "Investment classes? They have those?"

Ann nodded. "Yes. And I hate math. So if I can do them, anyone can."

"You make it sound so logical and easy," Cal declared.

"I think anything we want is just a decision or two away. Fear is what holds most of us back."

Cal put an elbow on the table and leaned on it while he stared. "Are you afraid of me, Pretty Ann?"

Ann laughed at his teasing. Because it was funny the way he called her that, but she'd heard the sincerity in his request too. "No. But I am afraid of the things you make me feel. I haven't wanted a man in a long time. Frankly, it's not very comfortable at my age, especially when the man is so much younger than me."

"Younger? Thought you didn't like doing math. Why are you doing it now?"

His grin made her grin back. "Smart-ass," she said under her breath.

"You're adorable, and I really, really like you. Let's date for real."

Ann sighed and then shook her head. "I can't, Cal. My dating calendar is full for the next two weeks. I wish I was joking about that, but I'm not."

Cal's serious man frown nearly made her laugh out loud. She held back only because she was sure laughing at that moment would definitely hurt his feelings. Yes, it thrilled her a bit to think he might be jealous. Wasn't that also completely awful of her?

"Dates? You have dates... as in plural?" he demanded.

Ann nodded. "Yes. Coffee with Lincoln and dancing with Brent. Then... please God... this madness will hopefully all be over. Ask me to date again in a few weeks, if you're still interested."

Cal snorted. "I'll still be interested. But what if you like those guys better than me?"

Ann shook her head at his question. "Doubtful. But you can count on me to be honest about the matter. I would never string you along."

"That doesn't reassure me, Ann. Are you this matter-of-fact about everything?"

She thought about that for a moment. "Yes. I think I am."

"Alright then," Cal answered, scrubbing a hand over the evening beard he couldn't seem to avoid.

The ride home was mostly silent. Ann regretted now that she'd told him about her dates, but what was she supposed to do? Keep it from him? Hide that she was busy? It wasn't like dating Cal was something she truly wanted. Well, at least, not consciously.

She stopped in the driveway to let him out.

"Pull inside the garage," Cal ordered.

Not wanting to upset him more by arguing, she did as he asked. By the time she cut the car off, Cal had hit the garage door button to close it and walked around to get her door. Sighing, she climbed from the car, only moments later to find herself backed up against it, with Cal's legs preventing her escape.

With his gaze locked to hers, Cal pulled the car keys from her limp fingers and put them on top of the car.

"Okay, I admit it. I'm jealous about you dating," he announced, as if it was news.

"There's honestly no need to be," Ann said softly, not quite sure why she was being defensive or trying to reassure him. She didn't belong to any man. She'd made no promises. Two dinners? Friends had dinner together all the time. She and Cal might be considered friends now... maybe.

"The idea of some other guy touching you or kissing you does not sit well with me." Cal held up a hand when she opened her mouth. "I know. I know. I know. But I have to put it out there."

His admission stopped any rebuttal she might have made, but Ann wasn't sure why.

His lips pressing soft kisses by her eye, down her cheek, and behind her ear should probably have given her a clue. She didn't really figure it out though until Cal nipped her earlobe and made her gasp. What was happening gained all kinds of clarity when his mouth swooped to hers and his tongue slipped easily and silkily alongside hers.

Her hands were suddenly in his hair, gripping and turning his head as she kissed him back.

His leg slipping between hers felt so heady. The firmness of it made everything around them fade to nothing. Then his other leg was there too and her hips were sliding up the car until her legs were practically wrapped around his waist.

He leaned against her, pushing against her. Her chest rose and fell from the rushing blood through her veins. Then Cal stopped kissing her... he stopped and put his cheek next to hers... his lips close to her ear.

"There have been a lot of women in my life... temporary women. It is never, ever like this. Never. It's only like this a precious few times in a person's life, I think. I also think it's damn easy to forget that. Please don't forget this over the next few weeks. Don't forget that there's a man in your life who knows you're a treasure both to be plundered and cared for."

Ann didn't know whether to laugh or cry. Her voice was husky when she answered. "Plundering sounds really good right now. Tell me more theories about that."

Cal's satisfied laugh in her ear was followed by both his hands gripping her hips hard as he pressed his whole body against hers. She heard that frustrated moan again—the same sound one of them had made the first time they'd kissed.

Light, rapid lip brushes peppered her face, chin, and throat as he eased her legs back down until her feet were solid on the garage floor again. Hands ran possessively over her hair and shoulders, travelling down her arms until Cal held only one of her hands in his. He grabbed the keys off the car and tugged her into the house after him.

Not stopping, he headed to the front door, tossing her car keys on the console table in the hallway. He didn't let go of her hand until he was standing outside on her doorstep.

"Lock up after I leave," he ordered. "And don't fall in love with some rich guy before I see you again."

Ann didn't speak, didn't nod, didn't react. She just watched the man who'd set her body on fire start his father's freaking work truck and drive away from her.

Cal had now done the unthinkable. He'd frustrated her to a point where she was as grumpy as Georgia Bates.

Ann suddenly had a driving urge to make sure her friend suffered equally. Evil thoughts blossomed about how to achieve that goal. It wouldn't make Mariah happy with her, but it might be worth it for the revenge.

Normally, she wasn't a person who sought revenge, but she was facing yet another sleepless night because of this dating stupidity she'd agree to. She wasn't a two-timer or a cheat, but the dating mess was making her feel like one.

*"Don't fall in love,"* she mocked, closing the door and throwing the deadbolt.

The very fact that she was tempted to call his father and make Cal come back irritated the crap out of her.

She hadn't played this physical torture game with her husband. When she'd wanted him, she'd just always said so. That life decision was now completely validated by her irrational anger over Cal leaving her in this churned up state. She promptly decided there was nothing in the world worse than being over fifty and horny.

If she'd been her daughter's age, Ann might have wondered if it was far, far too late for Cal's warning about not falling in love. But she wasn't Megan and she wasn't young. She was a woman who should know the difference between sexual desire and love.

But oh how she was tempted to let herself believe sexy Cal was offering her both.

# CHAPTER SEVEN

"ANN?"

She looked up into the handsome face smiling down at her. "Yes. That's right. And you must be Lincoln."

"Yes, and I don't think I've ever been so glad to be me." Lincoln said as he slid into the seat across from her. His gaze lit with pleasure as it roamed her face and hair. "You look just like your picture."

"So do you," Ann said honestly... and he did.

She fought the urge to twirl her hair. Maybe because it had taken a long time to fix it for this coffee date. She kept it long because a ponytail or braid kept it out of her face much better. But curls? Curls were not that easy. It was an hour long ritual she didn't bother with often.

She'd also swiped on some mascara and lip gloss, but that was just because she knew Lincoln had seen her with all the heavy goop on in the video. This kind of worry about her appearance was precisely why casual dating held so little appeal. It was hard work to be attractive. Few men sufficiently appreciated it.

"Let me get some coffee. Can I get you something fresher?"

Ann held up her cup. "No, I'm fine. Thanks."

Smiling, he headed to the counter to place his order. Lincoln was exactly as Mariah had described him. He was taller than her, incredibly handsome, and just as nice as Mariah had said he would be. Unfortunately, she felt nothing in his presence except misplaced guilt.

She couldn't cook dinner or drink a beer without thinking about Cal. She'd relived the whole kissing by the car thing so many times that her body had started finishing it in her dreams—several times in fact—something that still embarrassed her.

Her face was flushed with her wicked thoughts about Cal when Lincoln Walker came back to the table. She smiled at his look of concern. "Sorry," she said, fanning herself. "It's a..."

Ann caught herself just before she lied and said 'hot flash'. The truth was worse than even such a comment in front of a strange man would have been. Blunt she might be, but she wasn't completely without filters like Georgia. She knew you couldn't tell one handsome man that another handsome man was making love to her every night in her dreams.

"It's a woman thing," she told him, with at least a semi-honest, apologetic tone.

"Ah..." Lincoln said with a grin. "Want to go for a balloon ride and cool off? I know how to catch the best breezes."

"Cooling off sounds very nice," Ann said, thinking of Cal again. What was wrong with her?

"It's a date then," Lincoln declared.

Smiling on the outside as she sighed on the inside, Ann nodded reluctantly. "Sure. It's a date," she repeated.

ANN POUTED AS THE THREE OF THEM SAT ON THE PLUSH, LEATHER stools surrounding Trudy's granite island. She watched her retired chef friend dish up some sort of slaw, sliding the small bowls across the granite surface when it was done.

"Eat that and hurry," Trudy ordered. "Crab cakes suck when

they dry out. No amount of roulade will save them, not even my special recipe."

"You have a special recipe for everything."

A surprised Trudy glared back over the comment.

Embarrassed by the escaped snarkiness, Ann turned and glared at the two giggling women who weren't being helpful at all.

"Looks like somebody's seriously churned up," Georgia said, chuckling around a mouth full of slaw.

Ann hated herself more when a proper stare down proved impossible. Georgia was in rare, impenetrable form today. "Anybody ever tell you that you laugh like the wicked witch of the west?"

Georgia laughed at the accusation… and even louder.

"*Somebody's churned up.*" Mocking Georgia's taunting tone was fast becoming a bad, bad habit Ann wasn't sure how she was going to break. "Well, for your information," she spat out in defense, "I am not churned up. I'm just… *torn.*"

Georgia swallowed and looked at Trudy. "My bad… Ann's *torn.*"

Trudy covered her mouth with a hand to hide her smile as she turned back to flip the crab cakes sizzling on the griddle.

All Ann could do was frown as the epiphany came slowly, but at least it did finally come. Realizing you're acting idiotic is a hard thing to accept. Admitting it to your know-it-all friends is a far worse fate. Lusting for Cal was now making her growl and snipe at her friends.

"Must you always mock my pain and agony, Georgia? You're the reason I'm in this sorry state. I hadn't even thought about men or dating until this whole thing with Mariah's business. I blame you for my insanity."

Ignoring all my complaining and Georgia's happy laughter, Trudy dished up the crab cakes, drizzled something amazing over them, then spooned a melon compote on the side of each plate. Another drizzle from a different bottle and the plates slid in front of us.

Trudy slid her own plate down the granite surface until it stopped in front of my seat. The best chef in Cincinnati leaned on the counter so she could look me directly in the eye. It was almost worse than facing off with Georgia. Almost.

"What's the story, sweet cheeks? Don't leave out any dirt," Trudy ordered.

Ann's frustrated groan over having to politely answer the person feeding her elicited an empathetic sigh in response from sweet Jellica. It, of course, elicited another old hag chuckle from Georgia, who was finishing up her slaw like she hadn't eaten in weeks. She gave them both the evil eye. They deserved it. In the end though, all the frowning and glaring only made them all laugh harder at her.

Frustrated completely, Ann turned back to Trudy. "I like the man Mariah fixed me up with. He took me up in a hot-air balloon. It was the most fun I've had in ages. Lincoln was great."

Trudy stopped eating and stared. "But...? I could swear I heard a *but* in there." She turned to Jellica and Georgia. "Did you hear it too?"

Their traitorous nods had Ann sighing louder. Her head dipped to her chest as her eyes closed. "But he's not the guy I want to sleep with," Ann admitted.

"Guys as in there's more than one? You mean, Mariah's fixed you up with two guys already?" Trudy asked, sounding intrigued about the possibility.

Ann's hand lifted and waved in denial without any prompting. The debate that had been raging inside her head was now completely out on the table... or in this case, out on Trudy's granite countertop. The crab cakes tasted like sand. She knew Trudy was going to kill her for not properly appreciating her food when she realized what a bad guest she was being.

"No. Mariah's just set me up with the one date so far... but yes, I do have a second date, a dance date... well, that's not the same really. No. No. You see... I think I'm falling in love with my handyman's son who's way too young for me. Only, I don't know for sure because it's been over thirty-five years since I was interested in a man like this. Not wanting to deal with this internal drama is precisely why I haven't bothered in the last decade. As bad I hate admitting it, Georgia's right. I am churned up, but I don't like myself in this condition. I don't want my life to change. Why should it have to just because I want sex again? I've been fine without sex for years."

Silence filled the kitchen at the end of her self-pitying speech. Mortified, Ann shook her head and lowered her gaze. Trudy reached over and pointed to the plate of barely touched food.

"Eat your crab cakes, honey. They're getting cold."

Ann sighed heavily. "They're wonderful... good as always. I'm just not very hungry today."

Trudy lifted a bite on her own fork, then paused. "Maybe you've just got the hots for the kid who made you horny. I think you need to sleep with him and get it out of your system. Every single older woman eventually has a fling with a much younger man. How old is he? Twenty? Thirty?"

"He's forty-three and retired from the military. He's working with his father to help out."

Trudy blinked, then laughed. "Forty-three and retired? That's not a kid, honey. Damn... maybe you are falling in love."

Georgia huffed. "No. Ann is not falling in love. She's just deprived. She was ogling Mariah's new beau while we were getting our hair done. Her hormones are doing the mambo. That's all."

Ann shook her head. "I was not ogling. I was joking with Mariah."

"She was staring at his ass," Georgia said with an eye roll. "And I happen to know that John's older than Ann's boy toy."

"Cal is not my boy toy. He's not my anything."

"Yet," Trudy said.

Ann released an exasperated sigh over hearing the same word Cal had used. "I'm trying not to act on this insanity. I'm trying to be logical about our attraction to each other. Lincoln is closer to my age. Why couldn't he be the one keeping me up at night? He's fun, successful, and interested in me too. Why can't I feel like this about him?"

Jellica, who'd been silent up till now, stacked her empty plates. "Ann, all that's really happening here is your repressed libido is waking up. A decade is far too long for anyone to go without sex. I went six years once. It was like being a virgin again. There was even some discomfort with penetration no matter how much I wanted it. You really do lose a lot of muscle tone in your vagina when you abstain for too long."

"Unless you Kegel," Georgia added, her gaze taking in the whole group. "I Kegel every day. Hell, I'm probably in better shape down there than I was in my thirties."

Everyone snorted at Georgia's bragging, but we also knew she meant it. Kegeling was a helpful exercise, and not a luxury for those of us over a certain age who planned on someday having a regular lover again. There was an unfortunate truth to the 'use or lose it' claims.

"I'm not worried. Sex with Cal never hurt in my dreams—not once." Ann's face flamed when she realized that she'd actually been foolish enough to admit that out loud. "That doesn't mean I'm going to sleep with him."

Hysterical laughter filled up the kitchen.

# CHAPTER EIGHT

"THANKS FOR SEEING ME," ANN SAID.

Mariah smiled and motioned to the seat. "How did things go with Lincoln?"

"He was just as nice as you said."

"But...?"

Ann threw up a hand. "It's enough to make a good woman swear. Am I really that transparent?"

Mariah laughed. "No. I'm a trained listener for what's not being said. Was the chemistry missing?"

Reluctantly, but being an honest person, Ann moved her head up and down.

Mariah shrugged. "It's okay. Lincoln said he had a great time too, but even though he didn't say it, I got a sense of him realizing the right attraction wasn't there for him either."

"Thank God," Ann said sincerely, lifting her hand to her chest. "The guilt was horrible."

"Guilt?" Mariah asked, laughing again. "It was a first date, Ann. You didn't break an engagement."

"I let him kiss me after our balloon ride. I don't do that sort of thing—not usually. Mostly I was just being polite. But the kiss was... perfunctory."

"Perfunctory?" A grinning Mariah repeated. "It's so much fun having educated clients. They come up with so many clever ways to tell me a date was disappointing."

Ann sighed. "My lackluster reaction to someone as great as Lincoln is not amusing to me. I feel awful. Lincoln spent all that money to meet me."

"Well, stop feeling bad. He spends more money every month on his private gym membership that comes with trainers who keep him in that great shape. Lincoln is just fine, Ann. I'll eventually come up with someone right for him."

Ann nodded, but she was still unconvinced... and still not able to stop thinking about Cal. She wanted to ask him to come over just to see if his kiss still had the same devastating effect. But that would be counterproductive when she was trying to convince herself her reaction was about her and not about him.

Maybe she just needed more dating practice. More dates might help her develop some objectivity. Maybe an older, more appropriate man might stop her from dreaming about making love with a too young, inappropriate one.

"Can I try meeting someone else in that group of guys?"

"Sure. I still have your folder here at my desk," Mariah said, opening a drawer.

Ann bit her lip as Mariah pulled out another sheet from the stack and handed it over.

"This is Greg Skyler. He's an accountant with his own business. He practices Tai Chi and meditates. He likes rock climbing and hiking. You're a great match physically. He's in his late-forties—so just a few years younger."

Pulling the bio sheet closer, Ann studied the man's happy blue eyes. "He's just as good looking as Lincoln."

"Yes. Why do you sound so sad about it? Don't you want someone as attractive as you are?" Mariah asked, letting her concern show.

Ann's head whipped up. "You think I'm as attractive as all these men?"

"Of course I do," Mariah said firmly. "I take every detail into consideration."

"Sorry," Ann said, feeling humbled by Mariah's confident answer. "Who knew I'd be having self-esteem problems at my age? I was perfectly fine until I started dating."

Ann was silent for a moment as she studied the photo, but the weirdness of it all got to her. "Why do intelligent women let men twist their insides into knots?"

"Because men give us orgasms?" Mariah suggested.

Fanning her now flushed face, Ann snorted before answering. "If that was all I wanted from a man, I don't think I'd be having all these misgivings about the handsome ones. I'm still trying to find the most suitable companion to sit across the dinner table."

Mariah smiled warmly. "That's a perfect way to look at dating. A suitable companion is exactly what I'm trying to find for everyone in my database. Orgasms are just an important perk."

It was still daylight when Ann got home from her dinner date, but only because she'd pleaded a headache and left right after eating. She had let him kiss her before they parted, just to validate her conclusions. Greg was a nice man, and nice looking, but he certainly didn't seem to appreciate her sense of humor. Her lack of response to his kiss told her everything else.

The hours she'd spent fixing her hair and makeup now seemed excessive for her botched evening out. It was that stupid video and the six pounds of stupid makeup she'd had on in it. With any date Mariah hooked her up with, she felt like she was visually competing with an image of herself that someone else had created.

So distracted was she by her regrets about the evening, Ann didn't register her son's car in her driveway until she pulled into the garage. At the curb sat a sleek, red sports car as well. She wasn't great about identifying models, but the car seemed way too flashy for one of David's part-time security employees to be driving. Most of the men he hired were former military or retired cops. They had normal cars judging from what she'd seen in their building's parking lot.

And why was her son at her house tonight? The garage door was fixed. She was sure Cal had reported that back to David.

She walked through the kitchen, but saw no one. A quick search of the house didn't offer any clues. Finally, she spied David in the backyard, pointing and talking to a nodding Cal, who was dressed up like he'd been out on a date as well.

Had he? The idea of Cal dating, especially after the way he'd kissed her in the garage, did not sit well with her. What kind of man drove such a flashy red sports car anyway? In her experience, the ones who were trouble drove that kind of car—ones who snagged skinny, bleached blondes with silicone breasts and filled lips.

"Stop it." A quick head smack with her hand brought on enough pain to snap her out of her idiotic, jealous thoughts.

But what had she expected? Guilt and longing did not mix well or allow a person any inner peace. Hadn't she already decided Cal was too young for her? Cal should be able to do whatever he wanted.

She was out running around, kissing other men. Cal had no idea she was going on Mariah's dates only because she was trying to avoid liking him more than she already did.

Since hiding out in her own house felt more foolish than her fit of jealousy, Ann took several cleansing breaths before heading to confront the two men in her life.

"Surprise. I'm here to foil your evil plans," she called out, walking out the back door still in her shorter-than-normal, black dress and heels.

Her son suddenly looked incredibly guilty. Cal, on the other hand, looked like he was going to drag her to the garage again, or someplace else private. David was so focused on her unexpected appearance that he didn't even notice Cal staring lustfully at her legs, but she sure did. The thrill she got from it had her calling herself all kinds of stupid under her breath.

"Why are you home? Megan said you had a date tonight," her son protested.

Betrayed by a fellow female. Why should that surprise her? Her so-called friends did it to her all the time. "It was just dinner," Ann said flatly.

Her son's grin widened as his gaze took in her clothes. He elbowed Cal. "Don't those look like date clothes to you?"

"They absolutely look like date clothes," Cal agreed, crossing his arms.

Uncaring that David had no idea about her and Cal, Ann pointed a finger at the glaring man. "You have no right to pass judgment on me, Calvin Rodgers. You're just as dressed up as I am. Are those date clothes you're wearing?"

David's stunned gaze now swung from her to Cal, as if finally taking in what the man was wearing. Her son was probably surprised by how rude his mother was being, but that just couldn't be helped.

Ann rolled her eyes when Cal chuckled. David missed that too, because her son's gaze was glued to Cal's clothes as he inspected the man.

"If you must know, I'm dressed like this because I was trying to impress someone," Cal said with total sincerity.

Ann rolled her eyes again—even higher this time. Curse Georgia Bates and her bad habits. They were obviously contagious. "Really? Did it work?"

Cal spread his arms. "You look like a woman who always tells the truth. What do you think? Do I look good enough for a date?"

Her narrowed, now irritated gaze had her son clearing his throat, trying to intervene... or stop a fight... depending on how you looked at it.

Needing to defuse herself before she said too much, Ann turned to her still mostly clueless man child. "What's up with the unexpected visit, David? Don't make me call Kendra to find out about your shenanigans."

David jumped and checked his watch. "Kendra! Oh damn. I have to run. I'm supposed to pick her up in ten minutes." He turned to Cal. "Don't tell Mom anything, no matter what she says. It's her Mother's Day surprise."

Ann frowned. "David, you know I hate surprises."

"Normally, but you won't hate this one. Be nice to Cal, Mom. He's a terrible joker, but a really nice man under those fancy clothes he has on tonight."

Ann looked at smirking Cal who ducked his head, trying to hide his amusement from David. She was tempted to say she'd already had a preview of what was under Cal's clothes, but what kind of drama would that cause?

Instead, she turned her cheek up for a kiss and accepted her son's quick hug before he ran off like the lying coward he was when hiding something from her.

She knew better than to ask Cal what this nonsense was about though. Men rarely betrayed each other. Unlike her daughter... but she'd deal with Megan later. She had creative ways of making her daughter suffer for such sins.

Cal waited until David's car backed out of the driveway and sped down the street before he spoke again. "You sure look fantastic this evening. Hot date tonight?"

Momentarily ignoring the question, Ann looked over her poorly landscaped backyard. Now and again she dug a hole and transplanted something. That's about as far as she ever got. Gardening was the one task her husband had done that she hadn't been able to absorb.

"I'm home early, aren't I?" Ann huffed out a breath and screwed up her nerve. "How about you? You're pretty dressed up yourself."

Cal put his hands in his pockets as he walked to her. "I got dressed up for you, hoping you'd be here, even though David swore you wouldn't be. The truth is I wanted you to see me in something other than work clothes and a tool belt for once. I've been told I clean up pretty nice."

She didn't want to stare at him, but her eyes wouldn't stay off his crisp blue shirt and navy slacks. "Are you wondering if how you look is worth the price of a ticket?" His low chuckle over her teasing sent her nerves joyfully jumping, especially when he stepped even closer to her.

"Actually, I'm wondering if I look good enough to kiss. You sure do."

Ann sighed and dropped her gaze from his. "What am I going to do with you, Cal?"

"Are you taking suggestions now? My list is getting longer and longer."

His cocky answer triggered genuine laughter. He was quick minded, good humored, and...

"You do clean up pretty nice, Cal. Want to stay for a beer?"

Cal reached out a hand and pushed her curled hair behind one shoulder. "Yes, I would love to stay for a beer. Would it scare you if I said I wanted to stay for breakfast too?"

Ann laughed. "Yes, it would. I don't have enough beer to help me see that as a good idea."

Cal grinned. "Okay. Can we at least dance in your kitchen? I love slow dancing. Do you like to dance?"

Ann groaned and then she heard it. That sound—that sound she'd heard twice before. She'd been the one who'd made it, and this time she wasn't even kissing him.

"I can't talk about this any longer," she said, picking up his hand and dragging Cal along with her as she headed back to her kitchen.

His laughter over her cowardice filled up her backyard. "What's wrong, Pretty Ann?"

She didn't answer him. She didn't dare. There was no telling what kind of nonsense would come flying out of her mouth.

# CHAPTER NINE

Beers turned into beers and nachos. They ate them during a lively discussion about ethical investments which to Ann meant putting her money in companies that were trying to do good in the world. Their conversation bounced around other topics while Cal drank a third beer. Then suddenly they were both just quiet. The comfortable silence was surprisingly nice... or at least it was to her.

Sighing after two minutes passed unbroken by words, Cal pulled out his phone. He thumbed through it until a soft guitar melody drifted from the speaker. He stood and held out his hand.

Ann put her hand in his and let him pull her, and her suddenly weak legs, out of her seat.

Two beers had gone straight to her head this evening... or maybe it was the smell of Cal's aftershave as he drew her body close to his. It was amazing how being held in his arms felt exactly like the place she was supposed to be right then.

He gracefully began to glide her around the room to the music. Darkness fell the rest of the way as they danced. Soon the only light was the one she'd turned on over the kitchen sink.

The atmosphere was not the beautiful restaurant Greg had

taken her to for dinner. But the man? This man was the right one in the right place at the right time. She felt light and pretty when she was with Cal.

And she felt happy.

She felt like maybe it was finally time to take the kind of chance she hadn't been willing to take before he'd come into her life.

Smiling, Cal dipped her with a flourish at the end of the song. When he brought her up, she removed her hand from his and laid it against his face.

"I had to kiss two other men before I realized that your kiss was the only one capable of making me feel what I was feeling for you. I'm sorry I'm not coming to you more experienced. I swear nothing I'm doing is to make you jealous. Do you believe me?"

Cal let a ragged breath out as his hands slid to rest on her waist. "Were the guys rich and handsome?"

Ann nodded. "Yes. They were both rich and handsome."

"Did you like them?"

"Only one of them," Ann said honestly. "But I didn't fall in love in with him." Cal's man grunt made her laugh. "What's with the grunting? I thought you'd be happy with that statement, since it was the last warning you gave me."

Cal frowned as he looked at her. "I am happy. I just wish I was rich and handsome. You deserve someone like that."

Ann ran her fingertips down his clean shaven jaw and over his perfect lips—lips that knew exactly how to kiss her. "You're the most handsome man who's ever looked at me. But more importantly... you're the man I want. I'm sure about that now. Sorry it took me so long."

Cal's forehead touching hers wasn't exactly the move of the evening that she'd been hoping for from him after listening to her bare her soul. Then she heard that sound again—that sound she'd heard when they were kissing. Only it definitely wasn't her making it this time.

Something wonderful burst in her chest and the sound she did actually make was joyful.

Her mouth was on Cal's before she could second guess the aggressiveness of her action. Even caught off-guard, the man she was kissing only needed a nanosecond to catch up. His tongue plundered her mouth for real this time with no hesitation. Hard, insistent hands lifted her against him and she went up on her toes to help Cal find the best possible fit.

The kiss got real serious then. Cal's knees bent until he could lift her up and let her slide down him. There was no mistaking the question he was asking with his tempting body, yet his kisses got lighter as he eased gently away. His voice was a whisper, barely loud enough to be heard over the music still playing on his phone.

"Tell me, Pretty Ann... have you figured out what you want to do with me yet? I think it's obvious to both of us what I want to do with you."

Looking at him and thinking about the many, many possibilities, Ann suddenly made that same soulful sound. She made that sound that she now and forever was going to associate with the man looking at her like she was... well, everything important in the world to him.

Her answer was to hold his gaze while she sank back to her feet. Smiling at him, she led a wickedly pleased and grinning Cal down the hallway to her bedroom.

JELLICA DIDN'T DO MORNINGS, SO IT WAS RARE FOR THEM TO GET together so early. The four of them were huddled around Georgia's dining room table sipping bitter brew her friend liked to pass off as coffee. Ann really wasn't in the mood to be making any revelations to them, but she hadn't wanted her friends to worry about her either.

She stared into her still full coffee cup a moment longer and then lifted her gaze. "Let me just get this over with. I slept with Cal last night and it was more amazing than anything I'd dreamed."

"Did it hurt?" Jellica asked.

Three sets of concerned eyes were turned her way. "Not really. Well, I got a little sore after the third time, which was very early this morning. I'm definitely going to have to start Kegeling to keep up with the man if this continues. He either has a lot more energy than me or I'm not getting things done for him as well I should be."

Silence greeted her honest answer. Humor kicked in and Ann giggled as she stared back at the open-mouthed women she called friends.

"Sorry. That was probably TMI. I know it's only this way in the beginning, but it had been a long while for both us. And you know, I'd forgotten how nice it was to be intimate. I can't believe I went so long without sex. I feel very lucky that I picked someone so good at it. Lord, the man has talented hands. Cal also kisses well and with the best sense of timing. All that experience of his is actually quite nice."

"Are you keeping him?" Georgia asked, getting to the information they all wanted to know most.

"I want to—I think. But I've got one more date Mariah set me up with that I've said yes to," Ann said, hoping Georgia didn't press for more information than she wanted to give.

Cal had not been pleased with her noble intentions, especially after her obvious enthusiasm for what happened between them. After kissing her senseless in her kitchen this morning, he'd left shaking his head before the coffee pot had even finished brewing.

But a promise was a promise in her book, and Ann always kept her commitments, even the uncomfortable ones.

Or maybe she was just a bad woman. Maybe all those years of being nice had culminated in her wanting to have her way now. In her mind, she was coping the best she could with falling in love so hard when it had been the absolute last thing she'd ever imagined doing again.

Plus, this next date wasn't like the others anyway—it wasn't even one she wanted—or one Mariah even expected to turn out to be a match. She certainly had her own ideas about it, but she couldn't tell anyone what she was planning. As a mother who'd raised two willful children, she well knew successful manipulation worked best on those who suspected nothing.

Ann held up a hand and crossed her fingers. "One last date and then everything in the rest of my life can go back to normal. Then I can think about what I want to do with Cal."

Trudy snorted. "Honey, three times in the same twenty-four hours is only normal in men under twenty. If that's what you've found in your forty-something younger man, you might not want to waffle in your decision about keeping him. Sounds like the man has it bad for you."

"I have it bad for him too," Ann said, worriedly biting her lip as she nodded. Why wasn't she throwing her arms wide in acceptance of what she'd found? Cal had been nearly all she'd thought about since the day she'd met him.

Trudy shrugged and then sighed loudly. "Seems like the good men either die on you or leave you for someone half your age. I say keep the ones that make you happy for as long as you can. In between finding those men, you can go years and years with nothing worth talking about."

"Or you can put your fate in the hands of someone like my daughter who thinks she knows what's romantically best," Georgia said sullenly. "I say—what's the benefit of letting someone else pick the man you take to bed? Because I've never figured it out. I don't think I work that way."

Ann chuckled at Georgia's complaining. "Mariah gave me a folder containing at least a dozen of the best looking men I've ever seen in my life. And best of all, those guys picked me first. It only took meeting two from that folder to know Mariah is brilliant at what she does. They were *nothing* like the hairy chested mechanic with the gold chains, who hit on me last month. The men I met were great."

"Except you didn't end up sleeping with either of those men my daughter foisted on you," Georgia pointed out.

Ann shrugged. "Well, no… but Mariah couldn't know about Cal. Meeting him was just…"

"… the way finding love is supposed to freaking work," Georgia said firmly, rudely finishing the sentence.

Ann started to argue in Mariah's defense again, but that wasn't even what this was about. Georgia had her own axe to grind with her daughter. Ann had been hoping not to have to chase after any severed heads resulting from that axe, but that was just the nature of friendship, wasn't it?

"I hear what you're saying, Georgia. I can see why you'd think that. After all, Dr. Colombo caught you doing a toilet repair on his way to see Mariah. Are you suggesting we hang out in *The Perfect Date's* lobby and waylay the best looking ones before Mariah hooks them up with twenty year olds?"

Georgia snorted and shook her head. "The opinion I have is definitely *not* about my stupid interaction with Hollywood."

"Isn't it?" Ann challenged, ignoring the nickname. "The man met you naturally. He asked you to dinner naturally. You only said no because of who and what you think about him. You're not even giving him a chance just because he's rich. Technically, the natural way didn't actually work in your case, but only because of *you*. It was nothing Mariah or Dr. Colombo did."

Georgia huffed. "That's an oversimplification."

"Is it? Cal isn't any better or worse than those two handsome, wealthy guys Mariah set me up with. Both were very nice men. I just want Cal in a way I don't want them. Why I feel like that is mostly a mystery to me, except that Cal makes me feel very comfortable just being myself."

"Because Cal is retired military and his father is a handyman. You relate on a financial level and probably several others. Hollywood doesn't have to relate. People work their asses off to please him… not the other way around."

Ann shook her head. "Cal's younger than me and he looks it. At least the other men I went out with were nearer my age. I say my attraction to Cal is entirely about my attitude. Either of those two guys I dated would have been great for me if I could have felt the same level of attraction for them. They were certainly willing to show me a good time and try to get to know me, even when I didn't turn out to be the right woman."

Georgia threw up both hands. "How could you be? Because the right woman for them is probably twenty-two and fresh out of college. Rich guys drive sports cars and dress for dinner, Ann. They like their women young and dumb and freaking obedient. Hell, all men are like that, but not all men can lure a sexy gold digger who puts out on demand. Someone great like you is just their backup plan."

Cal drove a sports car and wanted her madly, but she for sure wasn't going to share that fact, no matter how great it would have been bragging to her jaded friend. Ann narrowed her eyes at the unfairness of Georgia's running commentary, but decided to see this insane debate as divine intervention. It only helped her plans to have a good reason to force her friend to go with her Friday night.

"That's mean and you know it, Georgia. You're old, cranky, and cynical about love. And your daughter is so much wiser about romance than you're admitting."

Georgia didn't answer her. Ann leaned forward on the table and pushed a little harder.

"If you're going to make all these negative pronouncements— you old blow hard—you need to at least offer some convincing personal proof. Cal's taught me that's impossible without putting yourself out there and seeing how it *really* is. So come with me to this stupid fundraiser Friday night and check out this third guy Mariah has set me up with. Make an *informed* decision instead of just spouting a crabby opinion every two seconds."

Georgia opened her mouth, but Ann held up a hand.

"No arguing—I'm not finished yet. If afterwards you can convince me the guy's a rich loser, then I'll listen to what you have to say and never debate this issue with you again. But if you like him, even a little bit, then you can't say another damn word about

Mariah's work or what she does to find any of us a date. You'll just have to suck it up and be supportive to us."

"Why do you care so much about proving me wrong?" Georgia demanded.

"Because I may be more of a realist than you. Cal is a terrific man, and we're terrific together, but he's always going to be a decade younger. That is not something I can wish away with starry eyes just because we have great sex. Love changes. Sexual attraction fades. I have to know the man I commit to is going to like me and still want me when relationship reality sets in. At my age, this next relationship will likely be the last one I'll ever have in my life."

They both turned when Trudy cleared her throat. "My sister married a very wealthy man. He was a young widower when they met. They have two residences, a vacation home in Barbados, a cabin in Oregon, and they travel a lot now that my brother-in-law is fully retired. Her life is way more stable than mine. I'm still working some and have responsibilities when I'm not, even though I'm nearly sixty. She's older than me and living with a nice person she still loves after nearly forty years of being married to him. My brother-in-law's money is making my sister's golden years truly golden. I think Ann's right to do all the reality checks. One of Mariah's wealthy clients could be a wonderful husband to spend the rest of her life with."

Georgia's gaze moved between Trudy's and Ann's. "How am I considered the jaded one here? You two think having money fixes everything. Well, it doesn't. Look at Mariah and her cheating ex."

Ann gave Georgia a chastising look. "That's not what either of us said. And stop trying to divert the discussion. If you aren't brave enough to take my dare for Friday, just say so."

"You've been a real pain in the ass lately," Georgia snapped.

Crossing her arms, Ann glared. "I'm not the only one. Admit you might be wrong and you can stay home."

"No."

Trudy chuckled, as did Jellica, who'd been remarkably silent for most of the discussion.

Ann grinned. "So are you coming? It's formal. You'll have to find a sexy black dress and put on makeup again. Looking like a hag will be considered cheating. You have to look your best and be your most charming. My date's rich men friends have to at least believe you like them a little bit or the dare is cancelled."

Ann didn't look away when Georgia glared at Trudy and Jellica for laughing. Any show of weakness would give Georgia an excuse to back out.

"Fine. I'll go. But I think this is stupid."

Ann shrugged. "So? That's exactly what I said when you got me to agree to this dating nonsense in the first place. Consider this dare my way of getting even. The makeover didn't count because that new haircut took a decade off your face. You should let your daughter make all your hair decisions."

Georgia's exaggerated eye roll set them all laughing at her irritation and Ann couldn't have been happier. Getting Georgia to go with her to the fundraiser dance had worked out better than she'd hoped.

Now she needed to focus on the second part of her plan.

# CHAPTER TEN

ANN TRIED NOT TO LAUGH WHEN THE TWENTY-SOMETHING CAFETERIA worker showed her to a table in a remote corner. Who had a reserved seat in a medical building's cafeteria? Apparently, the doctor who owned the whole place did, which shouldn't have surprised her. She was also told her "date" had taken the liberty of ordering lunch for both of them.

Thinking about what kind of person would do all that, Ann frowned as she sat at the non-descript table waiting for him to appear. If the man thought he was going to treat Georgia Bates so cavalierly, Dr. Brentwood Colombo, too-rich-for-his-own-good plastic surgeon, would need to hire a proctologist to remove Georgia's foot from his handsome butt after she'd kicked it.

After ten minutes went by, another cute cafeteria worker brought a basket of crackers to the table along with a tray containing two gourmet salads. Ann highly doubted the healthy greens with sprinkles of goat cheese and almonds had been assembled in the kitchen of a place sporting laminate table tops and plastic seats.

Moments later, a carafe of tea with mint leaves was delivered, along with two glasses full of chipped ice.

Having been raised to be polite, Ann ignored the salad and instead opened a package of crackers to nibble. It would stave off her hunger enough until her now very late date showed up. Luckily, she didn't have anything in her mouth when the man finally appeared in the cafeteria doorway. All it had taken was one look to completely understand why Georgia had nicknamed him Hollywood.

Females swarmed him with welcoming smiles and happy chatter. Some even offered hugs which he returned in kind with no holding back. Their reactions were understandable given the way he looked. Slightly taller than most women, Brentwood Colombo wore a custom fitted suit that matched his still nearly black hair color. He had gray temples instead of Cal's striking silver ones, but the drabness just created a contrast for his clear skin and clearer eyes. The man was clean shaven with a polished white smile that shone all the way across the room.

In all ways, he was sinfully handsome, but his allure was more than that. He seemed to genuinely take an interest in every woman who spoke to him. He asked questions, laughed at teasing, and gave each and every one of them a caring smile.

In short... the man was the polar opposite of Georgia Bates.

If Trudy and Jellica could see what she was seeing, they'd be just as astounded as she was that their cranky pants friend had enticed this incredible looking man into asking her out. Ann shook her head to dislodge her shock. The last thing she needed was to be less than confident about fostering the man's relationship to Georgia. But for the first time since this idea had occurred to her, she did wonder if she was in over her head.

So was Georgia if she really liked him... which could explain her friend's determination to run the other way.

Sighing in resignation when the hostess put a hand on his arm and pointed at her, Ann plastered a welcoming smile on her face to greet him. She really had no right to judge Georgia's reaction when she was just as contrary. Looking the handsome man over as he got closer and closer, all she could think is that he still fell short compared to a grinning, teasing Cal who couldn't seem to keep his hands off her. If this hadn't been her last date, feeling this level of ambivalence about such a good-looking man her age would have called a halt anyway.

"Hello," Ann said cheerily, deciding to hide the discomfort of her personal epiphany with a friendliness she wasn't yet feeling. She stood for introductions, totally stunned when he leaned in for a quick hug, smelling just as good as he looked.

"Hi Ann. I'm Brent. So sorry to keep you waiting. I had a patient who didn't come out of post-op as quickly as I'd hoped."

"No, worries. I just got here," Ann lied, quickly giving him points for apologizing.

"Sit... please," Brent said, taking the opposite chair. "I took the liberty of ordering in for us. The food here in the cafeteria is unfortunately basic. I wanted to do a little bit better for our lunch so I had them pick up catering for us."

Feeling churlish now in the face of his genuine niceness, Ann smiled. "That was very thoughtful of you."

Brent chuckled. "But...?"

"Beg your pardon?" Ann said, one eyebrow raised. His grin dared her to not answer. Her husband had always said she was hard to read, but lately she felt like she had an "Ann's Private Thoughts" billboard running across her forehead.

Brent studied her for a few moments. "*But...* don't surprise me again," he joked, his grin growing wider. "The hesitation was implied by the slight frown you worked hard to hide from me when you answered so politely. I normally don't buy food for complete strangers, but in my defense, it seemed better to risk your irritation than feed you a deli sandwich with chips."

A snort of surprise slipped past Ann's defenses. "You're safe. Saying rude things to a handsome and very thoughtful lunch date would be completely terrible of me, wouldn't it?"

"Perhaps, but I prefer honesty in my relationships. Don't you?"

His self-deprecating shrug and apologetic smile were boyishly charming. Ann giggled at the contrast of it with the rest of his appearance. Poor Georgia. This man was never going to give her enough to complain about on a regular basis. He was just as charming as Mariah had said... not to mention very sharp and knowledgeable about women. He really might be her friend's perfect match.

Ann's candid laughter filled the space between them. Brent shrugged again, obviously unconcerned about the impression he was making on her. She liked him for that... and she was starting to really like the idea of him dating her grumpy friend.

Her original plan bloomed to life again with even more possibilities.

"How much honesty are you wanting from me?" Ann asked, unable to stifle her merriment. His wince made her laugh again. "Tell me something, Brent... can you crank that boyish charm down a few notches? Or is it just too natural to turn off?"

"The latter, I'm afraid," Brent answered.

Ann nodded, but the smile on her face never faltered. "Okay. Here's my honesty. I only said yes to this lunch date so I could check you out because I sincerely care about my friend, Georgia."

"Georgia who?"

Her mouth dropped at his question. Unbelievable. Either he didn't know her name, or worse, he didn't remember. "Georgia... as in Georgia Bates. Surly woman who fixes things?" His continued blank stare had her narrowing her eyes. "Mariah's mother? The woman you asked out in a bathroom?"

"Oh. *Her*," Brent said quietly, grunting before laughing. "You're talking about Ms. Plumber with the perky breasts."

Ann burst out laughing at his description—this time drawing the attention of the entire room to them. "You seriously didn't know her name, did you?"

Brent shook his head. "No, and Mariah wouldn't tell me. I thought about having her investigated, but I figured that would look too desperate."

Ann's smile was wide. Her laughter was from her gut, which seemed to please him.

"Georgia... Sweet Georgia," Brent sang, picking at his salad with a fork. "Sounds too nice for someone that sarcastic. She called me Hollywood. I liked that nickname a lot, especially with the wicked look she gave me that went along with it, but I don't think that's what she wanted me to feel."

Ann nodded as she continued to laugh. "At least I know we're talking about the same person. That's definitely Georgia."

Brent stopped eating. His eyes crinkled when he smiled. "I confess that I keep reliving the day we met over and over. Nothing I do paints our interactions in a better light. The attraction was instantaneous, but no matter what I wished had occurred, the truth is she didn't seem as impressed by me as I was by her."

"Oh, you made an impression alright. Georgia's told all her friends about you. In fact, you come up remarkably often in conversation considering all she does is complain," Ann added, giggling when his eyes widened at the news.

The red climbing Brent's face betrayed his pleasure over learning it. She'd given him hope about Georgia. Now she was very glad she'd come.

"So if you don't mind me asking—since we're being brutally honest with each other—are you still interested in her?"

Across the table, her handsome companion, who could likely have any woman he wanted, and who'd no doubt had more than his share, sighed so deeply Ann's heart contracted in sympathy. He looked away from her, the sadness in his eyes real and heart wrenching. But when he looked back, the sadness was gone and humor lurked in his gaze instead.

"I watched her spray herself in the face with toilet water and just deal with it. Cursing like a sailor, she still joked with me about her breasts winning a wet t-shirt contest. That top she was wearing became immediately transparent. My interest in the thin lace bra she had under it made me stupid. That's the real reason I couldn't think of what the water shutoff was called. Not one of my finer moments. I could tell I lost major man points with her."

"Don't expect me to throw stones. That kind of situation throws you off-balance. I kissed a man in my garage while he had me pressed up against my car. Very high school for someone fifty-three years old."

"Yes. Sounds like a lot of fun too," Brent declared.

"It was," Ann answered truthfully, her smile back firmly in place.

Brent huffed. "I could tell the contrary woman liked me when she saw me... and long before she knew squat about who I was. She dismissed her interest in me because of assumptions—that's how she lost points with me. I liked her 'No Bullshit Allowed' attitude, which usually translates into stuffy and boring, but she was none of that. Georgia reminded me of my wife in the best way possible. They're the two most passionate women I've ever come across... and I've met a lot of women."

"Which wife?" Ann asked bluntly, picking up her tasty tea to take another sip. Boy, was she getting brave.

Brent looked confused by her question, then his expression cleared. "Oh. My first wife. The others were..."

"Mistakes?" Ann offered, digging for a noun other than gold digging bimbos.

Brent shook his head. "No. The others were fine women, just wrong for me. I was trying too hard to push the loneliness away. I thought marrying was the fairest way to handle what I felt."

Ann studied his face and only saw sincerity in his eyes. That told her all that she'd come to learn. Out poured her story before she could question the wisdom of trying to make this man her friend.

"I didn't date at all after my husband died. Every potential man lacked one thing. They weren't the man I'd married and lost. Dating without the possibility of falling in love seemed futile, so I just didn't bother. But I totally understand why someone else might fill that loneliness with anyone willing to help out. I was stubborn in my refusal to date all those years."

"Well, you're dating now though. That's personal progress, right? Mariah will take good care of you."

Ann chuckled and groaned as she dropped her head briefly. When she raised it again, she shook her head.

"Georgia was the one who talked me into signing up with Mariah. I've gone out with matches she's found for me, but they were a waste of my dating time. All on my own, I fell for a man ten years my junior who is absolutely nothing like any man I've ever known. It's the craziest thing to feel like this about someone at my age. Georgia is a staunch advocate of this insanity being how love is supposed to work. She loves Mariah, but I don't think she understands how much normal people need her daughter's help."

Brent grinned as he leaned across the table. "At the risk of sounding like a schoolboy about what you're telling me, do you really think I stand a chance with her?"

Ann leaned toward him too, ignoring the interested gazes aimed their way. Conspiratorial plotting might look like an intimate conversation, but she and Brent were knee deep in plotting now.

"You don't stand a snowball's chance in hell, which will make your conquest all the sweeter. That's why you have to try to thaw the woman's heart. Georgia needs you to push her out of her grumpy complacency about love. You're the only man who's managed to get under her skin in the whole time I've known her."

Brent snorted. "After I met her, I couldn't date anymore... well, except like this... and I had no choice this time because I really do need a dance partner. I'm expected to open the event I'm sponsoring with a formal dance. My youngest daughter is in a snit at the moment and refused to help me out. Mariah hasn't let me down yet. So I'm guessing you really do dance."

"Absolutely. I am much more than a conniving, sneaky friend." Ann stood and held out a hand. "Stand up and twirl me," she ordered.

She smiled when her handsome dance partner grinned and stood to obey. She laughed as Brent tugged her hand, spun her around in an elaborate waltz, and then dipped her over his arm. The cafeteria workers laughed and started clapping. Charming. He was just completely charming. Cal was lucky he'd gotten to her first. She'd have found a way to like this one. Georgia Bates needed to count her lucky stars for that botched toilet job.

"How's that for showing off my dancing skills?" Brent asked, looking down into her face.

Ann nodded as he stood her back on her feet. "You have perfect form."

"Ballroom dance lessons—years of them." Brent turned loose, sat back down, and held a hand out to her chair.

Ann was no dummy. She knew what Brent was doing in not helping her into her chair. He was leaving the choice about the date completely up to her. She lowered herself in front of a plate of delicious smelling food that had suddenly and discreetly appeared at the table.

"So... you're really okay with Friday?" he asked.

"Sure. Can I bring a plus one?" Ann asked.

"The younger man? Sure, bring him along," Brent said, shrugging as he ate. "It will be my first threesome for a date. I'm only paying Mariah for you though. His time has to be volunteered."

Laughing at his teasing, Ann picked up her fork. She always seemed to bring out the wicked flirt in men. It was one of her best qualities, and thanks to Cal, had been put to good use recently.

"I was talking about dragging Georgia Bates along with me. Don't ask how I managed it, but she's promised to dress up and dance with two men there. You, sir, need to be one of them."

Brent whistled and then he grinned. "Hey, you're really good at this conniving friend stuff, aren't you? That's like giving me two dates in one. Tell you what... if you get her to come to the dance, you can be my new BFF."

"BFF? Even my children don't talk that way. How old is your daughter?"

"Twenty-five going on thirteen."

Ann made a face. "Perhaps it's a phase."

"Let's hope so," Brent declared. "She's finishing up her first divorce and her self-worth is in the toilet. I've not set a very good example for her."

# CHAPTER ELEVEN

ANN STOPPED OUTSIDE HER SON'S OFFICE DOOR WHEN SHE HEARD HER daughter's voice yelling at her brother. She looked around to see if anyone else was listening, but there was no one. Even the new receptionist was out... and thank goodness. Curse words were already flying. She knew that meant emotions were running high about something.

Being a mother, her primal urge was to intercede and demand they find peace, but first she paused to listen. She'd learned long ago that eavesdropping was a very useful way to gain information about the truth of things. However, in this case what she learned only gave her an urge to laugh.

"Did you even ask Mom what was wrong?" Megan demanded.

"No, I did not. I don't like to worry ahead of time. She'll tell us when she gets here," David replied calmly.

"You're like a too calm robot with no feelings. It's a wonder Kendra doesn't kill you in your sleep."

"And I think it's a wonder Nicolas still has use of his balls. You're man enough for the two of you. Bet you guys always fight about who gets to be on top."

"Shut up about my love life, David. This is about Mom. She

could be terminally sick. She could be broke. Any number of serious shit things could be wrong. The last time I remember her asking to speak with us was when she told us Dad was dying."

"Nothing like that is going on. Mom wasn't using her 'something's wrong' voice when she called. She was just using her serious 'I'm concerned and want to discuss it now' voice. That's a whole different thing."

"What the hell does that mean?" Megan yelled.

"*It means,*" David ground out, "that I've been around Mom more than you have since Dad died. I think I would know if it were something terrible. I don't sense that, so quit chewing on my damn ass. Go do something productive until she gets here. Worrying never changes anything."

Ann chuckled at how wise her son was. She crossed her arms and smiled about her daughter's loving concern as she stepped to the office doorway. "Glad to know you two care about me so much, but do you have to broadcast your business to everyone you work with?"

"No one's here, Mom. We sent them all to lunch early," Megan said, blushing. "Sorry. You weren't supposed to catch us arguing."

Ann glared at her grinning son. "Yes. My mother sense has been working overtime lately. What's your brother plotting to do with my backyard, Megan? I caught him outside planning something and he'd recruited help who refused to talk."

Her own eyes narrowed when sister stared at brother without speaking. They talked with their eyes now. She actually saw both making a quick decision to play stupid. It was disconcerting when they ganged up on her and did that. The only blessing was that they finally stopped swearing at each other long enough to help cover their mutual guilt.

Sighing in frustration—because they both were adults after all—Ann dropped her arms and stepped inside the office. She looked at her daughter. "Megan, I'm physically fine. I'm not sick or hurt or dying."

"Good," Megan said. "David and I were worried."

"No. Megan was worried," David corrected.

Ann glared at her son. "So you don't care about me as much?" Her son looked like she'd slapped him. David was all big growl and no real bite when it came to her. Being mean to him was like punishing a puppy for being a puppy.

Rolling her eyes at the drama she was creating with her offspring, Ann raised a hand. "I'm sorry, David. I know you love me. I'm just nervous about what I have to share with you two. It's making me act a little crazy."

"Nervous?" David repeated. "About what, Mom? It's not like we're fifteen. You can talk to us about anything."

Ann shrugged. "I know that, but I'm still concerned about how you're going to react to my news."

"Mom—we know you're dating. It's okay. We both think it's a good thing," Megan said.

"How good would you think it was if I told you I've fallen in love?" Ann asked.

"In that case, I would hope you picked a very rich and generous stepfather for us," David teased.

Ann pointed a finger at him. "I don't care how rich he is... or isn't. I care only about what kind of person he is and how he makes me feel. This man fills all the criteria I have for a companion. I'm merely being cautious with my heart."

David nodded. "Mom, I was teasing. I think it's very smart of you to want to know so much about him before getting too involved. Megan or I will discreetly investigate the man. We three will be the only ones who know what we find."

"Investigate him?" Ann said in nearly a screech, her voice ratcheting up as loud as her daughter's had been only moments ago. "Do you really think I'd fall in love with someone who wasn't a good person? God bless my future daughter-in-law. Kendra's going to need the patience of Job to deal with you."

Megan's laughter earned her a glare. When her daughter continued to giggle, Ann threw up her hands. It wasn't up to them to approve of the man her heart had picked. It was only up to them

81

to accept her choice. She pushed her hair back with both hands, groaning at how weird it felt to be talking to them about letting a man into her life.

"Okay. Here it is. I have met someone and I will be officially dating him soon. What makes me nervous is that he's a lot younger than me."

"Younger? Way to go, Mom," Megan teased, giggling over the information. "Is he cute?"

"No. He's not cute. He's handsome," Ann said sharply. "He's also funny and kind and a good sport. I like him a lot and I'm thinking this might get serious. That's why I decided it was time to tell you both."

David snorted as he looked at Megan. "Told you it was nothing bad."

"Oh, bite me," Megan replied with full snark before turning back to her mother. "Who's the guy?"

Ann thought about it for a moment, and then shook her head. "I'd rather not say for now. I have another commitment through *The Perfect Date*. When that's over and done, I'll tell you who it is. For now, he'll just be my little secret." She glared at her son. "No investigating, David."

David grinned before shrugging. "Fine. But I'd like to meet him before he spends the night with you."

"No… and hell no," Ann declared. "You mind your bedroom partners, son. I'll mind mine."

"Wow. Mom told you, didn't she? She must *really* like him," Megan said, grinning at her grinning brother.

"Agreed," David answered.

Ann looked between her annoying children before shaking her head. "I should have said nothing until I was ready to marry him. It would serve you both right to be clubbed over the head with my decisions. I was trying to be nice and warn you."

Laughing now, David walked to her and pulled her in for a hug. "Just tell me he's a nice guy and I'll believe you."

"He's a great guy. You're both going to like him," Ann promised, because she already knew they did.

David nodded against her hair. "That's the only important thing," he said.

A smiling Megan leaned in and kissed her cheek. "How much younger, Mom?" her daughter whispered in her ear.

"He's in his forties," Ann answered softly.

"Oh. Okay," Megan said, shrugging as she pulled away. "Here I was hoping he'd be our age so I could like beat the crap out of him. I'd also lecture him about you being our mother and not his sugar momma or any shit like that. I figured I'd put him on notice so he'd be too scared to ever treat you bad."

Ann closed her eyes. "Good lord. My daughter grew up to be Rambo."

Her son chuckled against her. "That's exactly what I told Nicolas before he married her. I said… 'Dude, you're marrying Rambo. Deal with it.' Of course, he just laughed at the warning. Poor bastard is so in love, he's blind to her every fault. There's no saving him."

"Gee, David. You really think I'm Rambo? That may be the nicest thing you've ever called me," Megan said, smiling at her brother.

Laughing, because there was nothing else a barely sane mother could rationally do with children like hers, Ann leaned against her son and counted her blessings. She'd done her best raising the two amazing humans she'd birthed, but this whole single parenting gig was not for the faint hearted. It would be nice to have someone in her life to run interference for her occasionally—after they got over their shock of course.

She was definitely going to have to warn Cal about her children's tendency to overreact before officially outing them as a couple.

# CHAPTER TWELVE

THEY PAID THE TAXI DRIVER FROM THE TINY BLACK CLUTCH PURSES slung over their black dresses, and then climbed out. Ann stood on the sidewalk as she waited for her friend to emerge. Watching Georgia get out of the cab in her formal wear was as painful as watching a butterfly fight its way out of a cocoon.

Sliding across the backseat had not been a graceful act. Once out and standing, Georgia had to tug her fitted dress back into place around her curves. The platform heels at least did the dress justice, but how the woman intended to dance in them, Ann didn't know.

Georgia did another undignified shimmy as the cab pulled away.

"I don't get it. All that shaking and your boobs never moved a fraction. How does that even work at your age?" Ann demanded.

"Isometrics," Georgia answered. "They're the wimpy woman's answer to pushups. Sagging breasts are unacceptable and must be stopped. Unfortunately, I've never found the equivalent to help my ass stay up—hence the underwear tugging."

Ann chuckled. "Was that outstanding boob dress just hanging in your closet waiting for this event to happen?"

"No, smart-ass, but that reminds me—tear the tag off it. I forgot it because the stupid makeup took me forever to put on without looking like a clown," Georgia said, turning around and lifting her hair off her neck.

Because of Georgia's platforms, Ann had to raise up on her toes to grab it. One good yank and it was in her hand. Georgia snatched it away before she could look at the price tag. Her snicker over her friend's embarrassment echoed between them.

"Whatever it cost, you look amazing," Ann said honestly.

"Thank you." Georgia looked at Ann's more full-skirted dress. "You told me it was formal and that you were wearing your ballroom dancing dress with the sparkles on it. I didn't want to look like your ugly cousin who didn't know how to dress."

Ann nodded as they turned toward the doors where two bellman waited. "Glad you mentioned that. Being a dance partner is precisely why I'm here—and the *only reason* I'm here. I have to help open the event with a dance. Sparkles just seemed necessary."

Georgia rolled her eyes. "Yes, and you told me all that like twenty times on the ride here."

Ann reached out and rubbed her friend's arm. "Well, here's something I didn't say—I love you, Georgia. Thanks for coming with me. Tonight is important for both of us. Who knows? You might run into a man you like here."

The glare she got for her declaration put a grin on her face as they entered. Georgia nodded at the bellman who could barely stop himself from staring at her breasts. Ann laughed as they headed to where the people were gathering in the ballroom.

THEY HADN'T TAKEN TWO STEPS INSIDE THE ROOM BEFORE THEY WERE spotted. The only reason Ann knew for sure was Brent's low whistle of appreciation behind them, followed by a reverent "Wow" from the sexy man.

She turned when Georgia did, her smile beaming to see Brent's gaze running up and down Georgia like she was a fancy car he intended to buy.

"Hollywood," Georgia said flatly.

Ann covered her mouth at the sight of Brent's beaming smile on hearing his nickname. God, she wished some of their friends were here to witness this too. She should have asked to bring them.

Brent walked up to a scowling Georgia. "You look amazing... and you're not even wet this time. But then the evening's just getting started."

Ann watched Georgia's body tense. She wasn't sure what her friend would have said because the band struck up a loud chord and some emcee announced the opening dance between Dr. Brent Colombo, and his lovely partner for the evening, Ann Lynx.

With his gaze still locked on Georgia's glare, Brent reached out and grabbed Ann's hand, tugging her along as they headed to the dance floor.

"If you run, I'll call you a coward forever," Ann threatened, accepting Georgia's raised middle finger as her due. She let a chuckling Brent pull her out onto the dance floor.

A sea of people parted for them as they headed to the center of the crowd. She barely had time to register all the men in uniform surrounding them. It might have been a good idea to ask what kind of benefit was being held tonight, but it just hadn't occurred to her.

Mostly because it hadn't mattered.

All she'd been focused on was that this was the last of these she would ever have to do and she was here for Georgia's sake.

Brent positioned them both into a waltz form and the clapping for their performance began in earnest. Ann smiled at him and nodded, letting Brent know she was ready. Lights dimmed around the edges, leaving the focus only on her and Brent.

Her dance partner smiled back, and then they were dancing and spinning. She knew the smile never left her face. Dancing was one of her loves and she never got tired of doing it.

Georgia was seething while swearing silently in her head. She should have known Ann was up to something, but now realized she'd underestimated her friend's ability to manipulate. And Hollywood? Now she understood Ann's repetitive insistence about her merely being a 'dance partner' for this date. Not that her friend didn't look like a million bucks out there in her sparkling black dress. She and Hollywood looked like they'd been practicing for a long while. Hell, maybe they had for all she knew. Ann had gotten damn good at keeping things to herself.

"Thank God, someone else got to be on display," an angry young voice beside her said.

Georgia looked down half a foot to see a woman in her twenties glaring out at the dance floor. "Let me guess… you were supposed to be Hol… Dr. Colombo's date?"

"Something like that," the young woman grumbled. "But I hate these things. I only came because he made me feel guilty about staying home."

Georgia narrowed her gaze on the unpleasant young woman. "That's my friend out there with him. Ann said he hired her to be his dance partner."

The girl's snort turned into a sneer as her gaze turned and checked out Georgia. The girl's eye roll and head shake irritated her into responding to the girl's rudeness.

"Don't roll your eyes at me, girl. I have shoes older than you. And what was that condescending look for?"

"Did he give you those perky Double-Ds?" the girl asked. "They certainly look like his best work. And trust me… I've seen a lot of it."

"You're a completely rude little shit of a person, aren't you?" Georgia laughed at her comeback. "And for your information… these boobs are my own, smart-ass. With the droop you've got started though, you're going to need his help long before you turn thirty. Make sure he fixes the frown marks from your constant sneering too. *Trust me...* men prefer saggy tits on a woman to a mean mouth any day."

She turned back to watch Ann and Hollywood finish their dance to a deafening round of applause. Hollywood's pleased laughter as he pulled Ann close in for a hug pulled something close to a growl out of her throat. What the hell? She was not jealous—no way, no how.

"What was that sound you just made? OMG, are you *crushing* on him?" the girl demanded.

"None of your nosy business what I'm thinking," Georgia said tersely, ignoring the girl who was also glaring at the beaming couple headed back their way.

"He only dates women my age, you know," she said with glee.

Georgia looked down in disgust. "Wake up, Ms. Obvious. Do you think this is news to anyone in Cincinnati? Though frankly, I think you could do a lot better than him. If you altered that 'poor me' attitude and smiled once in a while, someone your own age might be able to like you. Thinking the worst of people will only make you look like a hag long before your time."

"Well, you would probably know that better than anyone," she said angrily.

Georgia's belly laugh over the girl's spunky reply earned her a seething glare back, but their exchange put a grin on her face by the time the smiling couple reached her. She stared in disbelief as Hollywood turned loose of Ann without looking and pulled the young girl into his arms for a hug.

Her heart suddenly and unexpectedly ached at his sincere show of affection. Luckily, she saw the humor in the situation.

Ann, on the other hand, looked simply appalled by Hollywood hugging the young girl. Maybe she was such a bad person, but all Georgia could do was roll her eyes and grin wickedly. "Tell me something, Ann. Did you blackmail me into coming tonight just so I could watch Hollywood grope his latest bimbo? I do admit this is better than most reality TV."

Georgia chuckled at the three sets of startled eyes suddenly turned her way. One eyebrow raised as the girl pushed out of Hollywood's arms and glared at her again.

"Now listen here, you hateful old hussy…"

"*No, no,*" a deep, sexy voice cajoled.

The effect of his calmness was lost with Hollywood's hand clamping firmly over the girl's protesting mouth. He shushed her right up, but Georgia could tell it was only out of shock that he'd do such a thing to her.

Georgia laughed, then looked at Ann, which had her sighing heavily. "Stop chewing your lip. I'm not going to hurt anyone or cause a scene. I do want to leave though before I get tempted any further."

"Too late. You're already causing a scene," Brent said sharply, removing his hand. He gestured to the young woman held in place now by his grip on her arm. "This is my daughter, Henna. Henna, this firecracker is Georgia Bates. My dance partner over there is Ann Lynx. Ann was my replacement date for the evening."

"Your daughter?" Georgia repeated the information, staring at the girl. She refused to feel joyful that he wasn't dating her. "That certainly explains the snippy attitude problem."

"Listen, old woman…" Henna began.

"She's not the only one with an attitude problem," Ann said loudly, stepping forward to intervene as well. She'd suddenly had enough of trying to help romance along. Georgia was the most stubborn, cantankerous woman on the planet. What kind of man could possibly deal with that? Brent was too nice. "Cupid knows, I'm sorry now for my good deed. Let's go home, shall we?"

"No. No one is leaving yet." Brent was suddenly there, dragging a protesting, shocked Georgia out to the dance floor with him. "We need to talk."

"Turn me loose, Hollywood, before I knee you," Georgia hissed.

"Smile, Sweet Georgia. Pictures of us are probably going to be in the newspapers tomorrow since you're kicking up such a fuss," Brent informed her, not letting her say no.

Ann watched in shock as Brent pulled a still resistant Georgia into a tight embrace despite the faster song playing.

"Brent must like her a whole lot more than even he thought he did. No one should have to put up with Georgia's crap." A girlish giggle by her side had Ann's head turning. "Hi. Sorry. My friend Georgia is... no, I can't explain her."

The girl snorted and lifted a hand. "It's okay. I started the battle between us. She was just very savvy about getting even."

Ann nodded. "Savvy? Not a word usually used to describe my friend." Amusement cleared the young woman's expression of all anger. "Brent and Georgia like each other. I don't know why or how, and she's already refused to date him. I had this idea if... never mind. I don't know what I was thinking."

"Oh, I don't know... look at them out there," Henna said, lifting a hand to point. "Dad dragged the woman kicking and protesting to the dance floor. He never does anything like that... never. He's unfailingly polite with everyone. She keeps wiggling and trying to get away, but Dad won't let her. I'm... I think I'm in shock... maybe even a little bit envious. My ex barely showed anger when I caught him cheating. He just shrugged it all off like it was no big deal."

Ann's sigh was loud. "Men can be cold-hearted and with such ease. I've known Georgia for a decade. She's incorrigible, but also one of the best women I've ever met."

Henna stuck out a hand. "Hi. My name is Henna Colombo. Nice to meet you, Ann Lynx. You looked great out there on the dance floor. Too bad my father couldn't be crushing on you."

Ann smiled and shook the woman's hand. "Thank you for the compliment. I'm involved with a younger man. Your father and I could never be more than friends, though I will say he is very charming."

"Charming... yes, he is definitely charming," Henna said, turning back to the dance floor. She lifted her chin to the still struggling couple. "He's also stubborn and will do anything to get what he wants. I think that's going to be obvious to everyone after this little stunt."

Ann looked in their direction. "Even if what your father wants is a cranky, jaded woman who hasn't been laid in years?"

Henna covered her mouth when she laughed. "Well, she has incredibly nice breasts which she swears are real. I'm sure Dad likes that about her."

"That's how I heard the story," Ann replied with a smile, crossing her arms as she waited for the dance to end.

# CHAPTER THIRTEEN

"Turn me loose," Georgia ordered, for the hundredth time.

"No."

Brent shook his head, laying his cheek deliberately against hers. God, he smelled wonderful. It wasn't fair. "Bet that cologne you're wearing cost more than my house," she said bitterly.

"Glad you like it. You smell nice too," Brent whispered. "And stop wriggling against me. It's torturous."

Georgia stiffened. He was getting aroused? Because of her? His body, making hers move with his, was the only reason she didn't stop where she was and just stare at him.

"The last wrong woman I married out of loneliness was over forty—she just didn't look it. On my honor, I've never slept with anyone under thirty, though I have taken younger women on dates. And if you want the whole truth... I haven't been with any woman in two damn years. I haven't wanted to until I came across your quarreling, grumpy ass."

She was silent while she absorbed the information.

Did it change anything she felt? Yes.

Did it make her feel like dating him would have any reasonable place to go? No.

Back to zero in her logic, Georgia sighed against his smooth shaven cheek. "I'm sorry I fought with your daughter."

Brent shrugged in her arms. "Knowing Henna, she probably started it."

Georgia chuckled. "She did, but that's really no excuse for some of what I said to her. Do you want me to apologize?"

"Suit yourself," Brent said.

"Hollywood? Why did you drag me out here to dance?" Georgia leaned away to ask.

He leaned away too, his gaze falling instantly to her cleavage as he swore. Sighing, he pulled her close again. "No reason good enough for you, I'm sure," he said in her ear.

Working hard not to be charmed by his confession, Georgia fought back the sigh of longing that went all the way to her toes. He wanted her physically and she wanted him back, which meant she was in big trouble. This man would wipe his feet on her heart if she let him.

"My feelings about us dating haven't changed," Georgia said quietly.

"I know. So stop arguing and let me have these two or three minutes to pretend you might actually like me a little. It will help my fantasies later when I have to go to bed alone."

"Stop. I never said I didn't like you," Georgia protested.

"Doll, your expression says it for you," Brent whispered, moving against her until she moaned in his ear. "Feel that? That's nervous anticipation of how great it could be between us. That's how romance is supposed to work. I hear you're an advocate of natural attraction."

"You're confusing me," Georgia said, her voice nearly pleading.

"No, I don't think I am," Brent said back, "but I am probably scaring you, and I get that. So just let me have this moment. Okay?"

Georgia nodded against his cheek and closed her eyes, playing her own game of pretend.

WHEN BRENT KEPT GEORGIA ON THE DANCE FLOOR FOR A SECOND dance—a genuine slow dance—a still stunned Henna wandered off mumbling to herself. Ann stood there watching and chewing her lip as she thought about how this might or might not work out.

When she got home later, she was going to call Cal. She'd break something if she had to in order to get him to come over. She needed to see him to clear her mind. She needed to tell him how she felt.

Another man finally approached and asked her to dance. Nodding politely, she let him lead her to the floor. Around and around they went, her heart not really into it as much as she'd normally be. But she smiled… and told herself all this would soon be over.

She was leaving the dance floor when one of the men in uniform stepped close. She looked up and her breath caught. Her gaze drifted over him and how stunning he looked, especially with his jacket's belted waist and uniform hat tucked under his arm.

Not asking, Cal put his hat on, took her hand, and walked her back out to the dance floor. Ann closed her eyes, feeling the deepest of pleasures when he pulled her into his arms and held her close.

"Surprised to see me?" he asked.

Ann nodded against his shoulder. "Yes. I'm supposed to be the date of the man dancing with my friend Georgia. I knew they liked each other so I was trying to hook them up."

Cal nodded against her hair. "Everyone can tell they like each other. What's their problem?"

Ann sighed. "I think Georgia doesn't think she's good enough for him. Brent has money, status, and a high profile job. She was a military housewife who worked part-time jobs everywhere they were stationed. She told me she never stayed in one place for more than a few years until her husband retired." She pulled away. "Why are you here?"

"Colombo does pro bono work on injured vets. That's what this fundraiser is about. It's to thank him."

"Oh," Ann said in a whisper. "I had no idea. All Brent said to me was that he needed a dance partner. I didn't even think to ask why."

Cal cleared his throat. "Well, he got a great one. You looked amazing when you were dancing with him."

"Thank you. This is that last date commitment I told you about."

"Yeah... I got that."

Ann tipped her head at his odd tone and saw Cal force a smile to his lips. His solemn look made her stomach clutch in anxiety. "What's wrong?" she asked.

Cal cleared his throat again. "You know what occurred to me when I watched you dancing? I figured out that the only thing stopping you from having this life is you, Ann. I know the kind of life you could have with someone like Colombo and the opportunity to meet men like him keeps knocking on your door. You really need to give the rich guys in your folder a fair chance to win you over."

Ann pulled away to search Cal's face. What she saw there caused her to stop moving. "I don't understand. What are you trying to tell me, Cal?"

Cal stopped too, cupping her cheek with his hand. "I'm trying to say that I don't think we should see each other anymore. Let your friend's daughter fix you up with someone who can give you a life I know I never will be able to. Stuff like this..." Cal looked around. "You need to dress up and go to dances. You need to be shown off. That's the kind of life you deserve."

"Are you breaking up with me?" Ann asked in surprise, her brain trying its best to take it in.

Her heart though was in total denial. This man... this man was the one she'd been waiting for. Now he was just going to walk away from her because of some strange idea in his head.

"I'm sorry," Cal said softly, kissing her on the cheek. "I thought about this every time you went out on one of your dates. Seeing you tonight made me realize how right I was to be concerned. I genuinely believe this is for the best."

"The best for whom?" Ann asked, but Cal just shrugged and shook his head.

Stunned to silence by his quiet resolve, she let Cal lead her off the dance floor. Dropping her next to an equally stunned looking Georgia, Cal brushed his lips gently over hers, tipped his hat to Georgia, Brent, and Henna, and then walked away.

It was so very civil... and felt so very final.

Ann blinked rapidly, the pain starting to set in at last. She was numb, but Georgia's hand gripping her arm pulled her back to reality.

"Who was that?" Georgia demanded.

"Command Sergeant Major Calvin Rodgers," Ann said softly.

"Cal?" Georgia said in surprise. "Your Cal?"

Ann snorted. "Apparently not any more. Cal just broke up with me while we were dancing. I need a bathroom break, Georgia, and then I'll be ready to leave. Sorry I dragged you here."

Not looking at any of them, Ann walked away with all the dignity she had left, which wasn't much, but she was hoping it would last until she got home.

"So that's Ann's younger man. Rodgers seems like a good guy," Brent commented.

Georgia rolled her eyes. "Good? He just broke her damn heart. Good guys don't do that, Hollywood."

"Your friend is so nice. She's pretty and funny. Men can be such total shits," Henna declared, glaring at the door Cal Rodgers left through.

Georgia glared at Brent and smacked his arm. "Go after him, Hollywood. Set the stupid idiot straight. He probably saw her dancing with you and lost it. Military men are like that. Under his impressive uniform, Cal Rodgers is probably just as stupid as any other male."

"Ow… no hitting!" Brent complained, rubbing his arm.

Henna looked at her handsome father, who she was now seeing in a whole new light. "I agree, Dad. I think you need to help. Ann did you a favor. It's not her fault how good you two looked dancing together."

"Roger's ill-formed opinion is not my fault." He glared at Georgia. "Did anyone ever tell you that you're crazy?"

"Yes. My daughter, the infamous Dr. Bates who created this mess, tells me that all the time, but I'm also right. Don't let that stiff backed man get away with this shit," Georgia ordered, shoving on his arm to push him toward the door.

Brent took a step automatically, then stopped. He turned back and smiled, seeing how this good deed could work in his favor. He knew Ann would be proud. "Date me," he ordered. "Date me and I'll chase the man down. I'll even make sure he goes crawling back to Ann. I'm very good at guilt trips. Ask Henna."

Georgia fisted hands on her hips and made a low threatening sound.

"Say it, Sweet Georgia," Brent ordered, refusing to leave until she did.

"*One*," she yelled at him. "One damn date, Hollywood. That's all."

"Tell Mariah. She'll never believe it unless you tell her yourself."

"No," Georgia declared.

"Tell your daughter you want to date me. If you don't say I bribed you, I'll pay your daughter's fee and give her a glowing referral to all the wealthy single men I know. That will keep us both honest."

Georgia growled again. "Fine. I'll tell her tomorrow. Now go!"

Smile at full wattage, a laughing Brent took off out the door nearly running.

Georgia released a pent-up breath. "And that's precisely why I hate this romance shit."

Giggling beside her had Georgia's head turning. She'd all but forgotten the girl was there. "Sorry about that. His smugness irritates me."

"No, it's okay. I hate this romance shit too, but watching you guys has been very entertaining tonight, and oddly... hopeful," Henna said, sounding surprised.

Hanging her head and groaning, Georgia went to round up her no-doubt weeping friend.

# CHAPTER FOURTEEN

"MOM? I DIDN'T KNOW YOU WERE COMING BY."

"It was an impulse, but I need a minute of your time, Mariah. This won't take long."

Mariah stared at her agitated mother who'd obviously blasted past Della because her assistant would have warned her. At least she hadn't been with a client.

"I…"

Della suddenly appeared behind her mother. Mariah smiled at her irritation. "It's okay, Della. We're fine."

Looking unsure, Della crept away, but not before glaring at her mother's back. Amused, but wanting to get to the bottom of things, Mariah turned her attention back to her mother. "Want to sit down? I have a few minutes."

Georgia shook her head. "No, and I can't believe I'm here to say this. If it was for anyone else but Ann, I wouldn't do it."

"What's wrong? Is something wrong with Ann?"

Knowing her daughter was still clueless about Calvin, Georgia shook her head and lied. "No. Ann just convinced me to be more open-minded. You can set me up with Hollywood. I… I want to date him."

Mariah tilted her head. "Are you sure?"

Georgia lifted both hands. "Don't I seem sure?"

"Not really—no."

Georgia used her hands to push her hair back. "Well, I am. So what do I need to do? Didn't I finish the stupid bio stuff already? Is there anything else?"

Mariah shook her head. Shock didn't even begin to cover what she was feeling. "Nothing. You don't need to do anything else. I'll set up a coffee date with Brent so the two of you can talk and make plans for your... date."

"I'd rather eat nails than have coffee with him, but okay. If that's how this has to work, I'll do it."

"Mom? Are you really sure about this? Maybe we need to talk before I..."

Georgia shook her head. "No... no need. I'm absolutely sure. I'm just... I'm just very nervous."

"It will all be fine, Mom. Brent's a very nice guy. Everyone says he's a fun date."

The snort escaped. It couldn't be helped. "I just bet they do," Georgia said.

"Mom... that does not sound like you really want to date him. What's going on?"

Georgia glared at her daughter. It figured the woman she raised to be skeptical would need blood before believing her. "I'm tired of people calling me grumpy and cranky and all sorts of other unflattering things. So I'm going to date the bastard and see if it makes any damn difference. Is that okay with you or not?"

"Sure," Mariah said cautiously. "I'll check with Brent for some times that he's free and get back to you."

"Fine. Do that," Georgia declared.

Rolling her eyes over the man who'd successfully blackmailed her into dating him, Georgia left before she blurted out the whole story.

~

ANN POKED AT THE STILL PAPER WRAPPED DELI SANDWICH. SHE'D LET some man into her life, and now that he was gone, she couldn't eat. This felt a lot like when her husband died only worse because she knew Cal was still walking around somewhere not wanting to be with her.

"He's just a stupid man. Eat, damn it," Georgia ordered, slapping her hand on her dining table and making them all jump. "Trudy drove all the way to West Chester to get these organic sandwiches because she knew they were your favorite."

Ann nodded. "You're right. I know you're right. I should eat and not care, but I don't know how to do that."

Huffing, Georgia stopped eating. "You did nothing wrong. If this is anyone's fault, it's Hollywood's."

Snorting at the unfairness of that accusation, Ann unwrapped her sandwich. "This is not Brent's fault. Or Mariah's. Or yours. I don't even think it's mine. Cal saw me dancing and got some stupid idea in his head that I needed a man with money. Should I even care about someone that dumb?"

"Yes," the three women sitting with her answered.

"Why?" Ann demanded, stunned at the unanimous answer.

Trudy held up a finger. "The man gave you orgasms. Remember the three in one sleepover thing you shared. Good sex is the foundation of a good relationship. Hard as hell to find too."

"And he's romantic. You told us he danced with you in your kitchen. That's an unusual man," Jellica added.

"Your boy toy's a bonehead about how women really think, but you shouldn't kick a man to the curb for one dumbass decision," Georgia said, biting into her sandwich. She chewed and swallowed. "It's okay though... I sent Hollywood after Cal to set him straight."

Ann gasped at the thought. "Georgia... you didn't."

Georgia pushed the rest of the pickle slice into her mouth and nodded.

Groaning, Ann bit into her sandwich. "Now Brent's involved in my craziness. This just gets worse and worse." She chewed and chewed, swallowing out of self-defense so she wouldn't choke on her anxiety. "Brent barely knows me. All I did was dance with him."

"I agree he's more self-serving than altruistic, but someone needed to set the man straight. The truth is Hollywood blackmailed me into going out with him. I said yes to get him to help," Georgia reported calmly.

Ann stared at Georgia. They all did. "You're going out with Brent?"

Snorting, Georgia nodded. "Yes. Handsome bastard gave me no choice."

"Unbelievable," Ann said, shaking her head.

Georgia shrugged. "What's really unbelievable is that Hollywood missed catching your bozo boyfriend after the dance. You and I were gone before he could tell me. But he said today that he was not giving up on tracking Cal down. I gave him Stan's name and address—figured I might as well help out. Hollywood knows I won't go out with him unless he keeps his word and makes Cal come crawling to apologize.

"Wow, Georgia. The man must really like you," Jellica said, sighing with envy.

Georgia refused to think about their dancing and his interest in her body. "I think all I am is a challenge. He's used to women falling at his feet. I don't intend to, but whatever... I can play the game to help a friend."

"If this is supposed to be how true love works, then Cupid is stupid," Ann declared, taking another bite. "These are good, Trudy. Thank you. It's the first food I've enjoyed at all in a couple days. I can't even drink a beer now without thinking of him. God, I can't stand being this pathetic."

"My pleasure, sweetie... and you're not pathetic," Trudy said.

"Well, I know one thing," Ann said, lifting her chin. "If Calvin Rodgers doesn't want me anymore, there's at least nine other guys in Mariah's folder. I'm not going back to living my sad widow life before he came along. It may take me a while to find another man I want to sleep with, but life is far too short to live it alone."

She turned then and looked only at Georgia. "That's why I'm glad you're going out with Brent—no matter how things turn out. Falling in love again is worth the risk, Georgia, even when it doesn't last. I can't tell you how much Cal changed my life. I may still be hurt and angry, but I can see the good he did for me."

Georgia laughed. "You're such an optimist. Maybe that will eventually rub off on me. Want to stay over? That way, when Hollywood reports in, you'll be here to hear the news first hand. Good. Bad. Or otherwise."

Ann shook her head. "No, thanks. I already know Brent's not going to change Cal's mind. Did your military husband ever change his mind once it had been made up about something important?"

"No," Georgia admitted. "I just learned how to effectively work around his stubbornness. You could learn to do the same. I have faith in you."

Ann shook her head. "My gut is telling me that nothing Brent does and nothing you do is going to make any difference. Cal broke up with me for what he considers to be my own good. You can't fight that kind of thinking."

"Then Cal's truly an idiot," Georgia stated, not blinking as she held Ann's gaze.

Ann dropped her head, nodded, and wadded up her napkin. She rolled the majority of her sandwich back into its wrapper. "I'll eat this later. I'm going to go home, have another good cry, and hopefully wake up tomorrow in a much better frame of mind."

After hugs and more hugs, Ann peeled herself away from her friends and went home.

~

CAL SILENTLY LOADED SUPPLIES IN THE TRUCK BED FOR THE TWO JOBS he was doing tomorrow. The man was clearing his throat before

Cal even saw him standing ten feet away. It was hard to believe he'd gone so soft already. Distraction in the military might get you killed. Distraction out here just let people you didn't want to see sneak up on you.

"Rodgers? We need to talk for a minute. I tried to catch you after the dance, but you took off before I could track you down."

Cal looked at the pristine doctor in his who-knew-how-many-thousand dollar suit. He understood the choices each of them had made had brought them to where they now were. He'd been mostly happy with his life until he'd lost the woman he'd wanted to a guy who had a life Cal couldn't even fathom having.

"Sorry. What did you need to see me about, Dr. Colombo?"

Brent put one hand in his pocket. "I need to warn you about your upcoming Proctology visit with Georgia Bates if you end up breaking Ann Lynx's heart. That sweet woman's in love with you, Rodgers. Ann told me so when we had lunch. The only reason she was at the dance with me was to be my partner after my daughter stood me up."

Cal shoved a box of siding into the bed of the truck. "Ann never said anything to me about love. And how is this any business of yours?"

"I figured you military types wouldn't scare off so easily. Didn't you hear what I said? *She's in love with you*, which makes Ann *your* business. Her friend, Georgia, well, she's my business. However, I owe Ann for my second chance. That's why I'm here to tell you that you need to fix your situation before that feisty woman decides to move on."

"Ann doesn't need me. She needs someone like you to take her dancing and out to dinner. For all intents and purposes, I'm starting over in my life. My retirement isn't going to go far in today's economy. Since I'm only proud of my military career and the fact that I can help my father, all I can do for Ann is get the hell out of her way."

Brent let out a jagged breath. "That's just ego talking, boy. Ann doesn't want someone like me—mostly because she thought she had you. True, Mariah has a folder of men interested in her. If she ever wants another man, they're going to be easy enough to come by. If you want, I'll just leave you to wallow in your misery. I'll tell the women you weren't interested in hearing what I had to say."

"Of course I'm interested, but Ann deserves more than I can give her. Wealthy guys like you can give her a better life. There's no reason not to just say that. She's been dating them all along anyway. You weren't the only rich guy she went out with."

"Someone your age ought to know by now that money doesn't make a man good or bad. Ann deserves someone to love her, not someone picking her off a shelf, which is kind of what Mariah's matching up feels like when it doesn't work out. Do you love her, Rodgers? Because right now I know Ann thinks you don't. Right now, she's probably home crying over you. That's what women do when their hearts get broken. They bawl and it makes their eyes all puffy and red. They hate that. Trust me. So get your ass over there and fix this while you still can."

"No. It's over between us. But thanks for coming by," Cal said, turning away.

"Fine. Okay. You're making a mistake, though. Losing the right woman can have a long term effect. I never stopped missing my first wife until I met Georgia. That's a long damn time to go without really loving anyone."

Cal turned and watched the man stride back across his father's rough looking backyard. What did men like Dr. Colombo know about the lives of average people? Very little, he'd guess.

It did surprise him that the renowned plastic surgeon had simply shown up here. How many appointments had he had to rearrange? Why would someone like Colombo do that?

He didn't for one minute think it was really about Ann, though the man did seem to genuinely like her.

Cal leaned against the truck bed and rubbed his chest. Even having the best of intentions wasn't making this easy.

His own body had been aching since he'd walked away from her. Worse still was thinking Ann would never again fix him dinner, offer him a beer, or drag him to bed. Reality had set in on his drive home that night, but part of him still felt he was right.

But what if Dr. Colombo was right?

What if Ann loved him and he had broken her heart?

That would be bad—very, very bad. He'd watched Ann smiling while she was dancing. Wouldn't she just go on and do that without him? She'd had no problem dancing with Colombo and that other guy who'd asked her. That's why he hadn't bothered.

The arrogant doctor had planted real doubt in his mind, even though he hadn't shown it to the man.

Now he was going to have to find out if Ann was okay, if only to remain sane. Cal only knew one sure way to do that, and it wasn't going to be easy.

# CHAPTER FIFTEEN

CAL HEARD THEM YELLING WHEN HE WALKED IN. HE LOOKED AT THE receptionist who shook her head. What fresh hell was this? Walking to the office door, he saw Megan pacing with balled up fists. David sat behind his desk frowning at the wood surface of it.

"I promised Mom we wouldn't investigate the guy," David said calmly.

Megan nearly screamed. "Did you not hear what I said? Mom's digging holes. You know what that means."

"I don't. What does it mean?" Cal asked as casually as possible, stepping through the door uninvited.

"It means that no balls bastard she's been dating broke her heart," Megan said, swiping a hand through the air. "Mom hates yard work. Hates it. Now there's like twenty holes around the yard. She says she's planting something, but she's not. All she's doing is digging."

Cal burst out laughing. Digging holes? "Maybe she's just prepping for spring planting."

"No," David said, frowning. "Mom dug a lot of holes after Dad died. Nothing ever went in them. After a year went by, I took a couple guys over there one day and filled them all back in."

"When I find the SOB who hurt her, I'm going to… well, I don't know what I'll do to him. Something legal, but very painful," Megan declared.

David's gaze turned his way. "The yard has been a sore spot since Dad died. She's been happy lately though, so I thought maybe it was time to finally do something to the yard. That's why I talked to you about putting a covered deck with a built-in barbecue back there. She's always wanted that, but Dad never would spring for it. This is the first time I thought Mom had finally put the past behind her."

Cal swore under his breath. He found a chair and sat in it. "Did your mother specifically tell you something was wrong with her and the guy?"

"Ask her," David ordered, gesturing to his sister. "Personally, I can't understand Megan's emotional ranting when she gets like this. I usually need her husband to translate her bitching."

Cal watched Megan glare at David. She looked like she was going across the desk after her brother. Ann must have had her hands full with these two.

He spun a chair around at an angle. "Sit, Megan," he ordered, using his command voice.

Frowning, the younger woman took the chair. Cal drew in a breath. "Let's just cover the basics for now. Did your mother say anything about what was bothering her? How do you know it was a problem with the guy she was dating?"

Megan shook her head. "Mom said it was.." Fingers raised in the air for quote marks. "…nothing I needed to worry about." A huff followed that. "She was covered in dirt and still digging. Her eyes were red from crying. Does she think I'm stupid? That damn younger guy she likes probably threw her over. Only the serious shit sends Mom after the shovel."

Cal looked at David. "Is that true?"

David's nod was brief. "Yeah. Every word about the serious shit is true. It sends her after the shovel."

"Oh, hell," Cal said. "This is really bad, isn't it?"

Twin nods and frowns more than answered his question. His mistake was growing in magnitude. These two tackled problems to the ground. If they were upset, something was definitely wrong. He couldn't keep fooling himself.

Cal looked at Megan and drew in a breath before speaking. "I swear on my life that I never in a million years meant to hurt your mother. I'm in love with her, Megan. Please don't hit me. I need my entire brain to figure out how to fix the shit storm I accidentally started."

David leaned across the desk. "Rodgers? Are you telling me that you and my mother...? Seriously?"

Cal nodded. "Yes. I fixed her pantry. Ann asked me to stay for dinner. So I did. I've been seeing her ever since. I kept seeing her even while she was seeing all those other men... which was why I had doubts."

"*Other men?* My mother was seeing other men?" Megan exclaimed.

"You know... *The Perfect Date* rich dudes from that service," David filled in.

Megan snorted. "Oh, them. She didn't like them. They were just her way of making sure..." Her gaze rounded to Cal. "She really, really liked you, dumbass. You were the only one she liked. She refused to tell me and David who you were. She also jumped David's ass for wanting to investigate you before she sleeps with you."

Cal sighed and put his gaze on the ceiling, grateful for Ann's discretion about their relationship. It meant he might walk out of David's office alive. Finally, he nodded. "Last Friday, I saw her dancing with one of her so-called dates. The man's suit cost more than my sports car. I panicked."

"You mean your ego did," David said.

"Yeah. Fair enough," Cal replied, shrugging as Colombo's chastising came back to haunt him again. "She looked so happy out there dancing. You should have seen how happy she looked."

Megan swiped the air again with her hand. "Mom dances with

anyone because she just loves dancing... even belly dancing. It was so embarrassing when I was a kid. All my friends in school knew because Mom used to teach classes to their moms."

"*Belly dancing?*" Cal asked, stunned by the images chasing through his mind. He rubbed a hand over his face, wondering when and how Ann might have chosen to tell him. His body tensed, tightened, and longed for her. His stupidity was becoming more and more clear.

"Get a grip, Rodgers," David ordered, smirking over the man's reaction to the news.

"How the hell can I make this up to her? I have to."

"Admit you're a dumbass and apologize," Megan ordered, crossing her arms. "Then let her rant until she starts to cry. Once she cries, then apologize again. That's when she'll finally hear you."

Cal stared at Ann's daughter a long time. "Okay." He glanced at David and back at Megan. "You two got any real problems with me and your mother?"

"Not if you stop acting like a no-confidence loser and make her smile again. God, I'm glad I chose the freaking Marines. Army guys are such wimps."

"Hey now," Cal said, glaring at the girl for the first time.

"I went after and married the richest man in Cincinnati. That makes me fully qualified to give you shit for not having the balls to go after my mother who hasn't dated in years. And David has to go home to an attorney every day—an attorney who can slice you open with words alone. You fall in love with someone, Cal... that's what you do... you go home to them and deal. My mother is a saint next to the people David and I married."

"Yes, ma'am. I agree that your mother is a saint," Cal said contritely, but with a smile blooming on his face.

He wanted to be angry at Ann's smart-ass daughter, but all he could do was laugh at her urgings for him to fix things. This could be much worse. They could both have just hated the idea of him and her.

"My being a wimp about your mother has nothing to do with the branch I served in. I just got cold feet when I saw her dancing with those rich guys."

Megan snorted. "If Mom wanted a rich guy, she could have dated Trudy Baxter's brother."

"Chef Baxter?" Cal asked. Everyone in Cincinnati knew the woman.

Megan nodded. "It was several years ago. Mom wouldn't even meet him for coffee. That's when David and I knew she'd shut down about men. There's been no one. That's how I really know you're the reason she's digging holes."

Cal leaned forward on his knees and dropped his hands between them. He should have listened to Dr. Colombo... well, he did in a way. That was the reason he ended up here.

"I was the one who broke it off. Getting her back is going to require a full out assault, not one of those ease into it things. I walked away from her. She's going to do the same to me... maybe more than once. I need to pull out the big guns right away to keep that from happening."

Megan stared at the wall. David stared at the desk.

Cal stood. "I'm going home and put on my uniform because I'm going to need to look too good for her to refuse. One of you needs to meet me at the house in an hour. Your job will be to let me in and then scram before the fireworks start. Sound like a plan?"

"Sounds like a suicide mission. Mom's had a few days to build up her emotional walls," Megan said.

"It'll be okay," Cal said, trying to think positively. He grinned at the two of them. "I'll bring my tool belt and big hammer with me for those walls. Maybe I'll impress her with my man skills again."

David's wicked look at him was followed by a snicker, which earned him a hard smack from his frowning sister that nearly knocked him out of his chair.

Cal chuckled and gave a head shake. "I don't know how you two work together."

"Neither do we," David said, laughing as he stood and shoved Megan into the nearest wall.

# CHAPTER SIXTEEN

Ann lifted the shovel and stabbed the ground with it. After the four hours of watering she'd done last night, the blade cut right through the dirt. She told herself the hard work made up for missing yoga and not taking walks. She told herself that it was soul reviving. Now she just needed to believe it.

Her thoughts kept roaming around without her permission, trying not to dwell on what had happened Friday. But it was hard to remember the last time she'd been this disappointed with her life.

Her husband's sudden death by a heart attack ranked at the top of the list, but right below that was a host of other things. Like maybe she should have found the money to enroll Megan in those advanced ballet classes she'd shown some interest in. Maybe her daughter would have turned out a bit more feminine, not that Nicolas seemed to mind Megan's assertiveness.

And wouldn't Megan have been more like her than she already was?

Well, screw that. She was glad her daughter was a hard-ass Marine. If Nicolas had sauntered away from Megan after she'd slept with him, her daughter would have gone after his insensitive ass and kicked it.

So why hadn't she gone after Cal? She'd raised two tough, aggressive teenagers, and mothered the tough friends they'd both brought home to her. Why was she afraid of demanding Cal give her another chance?

Sweat ran everywhere the harder she thought. She pulled at the back of her shirt and then at the front. Even though she wasn't hot, her bra was soaked.

"Stop it, Ann Lynx. You didn't go after him because Cal is as plain-spoken as you are. If he said he was done, he meant it. So stop mooning over the man and get your planting done. You've been putting the tough things in your life off for far too long."

The shovel hit the ground again, scooping out the wet dirt. Fortunately, she only needed a few more. She would finish what she started as soon as the hot tears streaming down her face and over her hands stopped falling.

TWO HEADS STARED HELPLESSLY OUT THE WINDOW, WATCHING THEIR mother dig into the ground with a viciousness anyone in their right mind would have dreaded facing off with.

"Oh shit. Look at her now. She's been working on this all week. There must be twenty or thirty holes out there."

"It's only fifteen, Megan. Stop exaggerating."

Shaking his head at their bickering, which was far worse than his girls had ever done, Cal stepped between them and peered out the window too. He swallowed hard when he saw Ann stop and swipe at her eyes. She was filthy and crying… and he knew it was his fault.

The guilt that tugged at his chest had to be true love. Nothing else explained how low he felt for causing that sweet woman any kind of pain or hurt. He'd have rather taken a bullet. Instead, he'd fired an unexpected one at her in a moment of blind emotional panic.

Megan turned her head to stare at him. "You look good in your monkey suit. Are you scared?"

"Thank you… and yes," Cal said truthfully. "I hope your mother thinks I look good. I'll need the distraction."

"She will," Megan said, turning back to the window. "We have similar tastes in men."

David glanced at him, grinned, and shook his head. They'd each gotten a little of their mother, but David was the most like Ann in personality. His calmness was watchful and caring. Ann's son might wait to see what played out, but the man would be there if needed. Of that, Cal had no doubt.

Putting his hat on his head, he straightened his shoulders and drew in a deep breath.

"Wait," Megan said, rising to stand.

She brushed invisible lint off him and patted his shoulders to straighten the line of his jacket. Cal's heart contracted when Megan threw her arms around him afterward and hugged tight.

"I hope she keeps you. It will be nice to have another military person in the family."

Cal's arms came around her without thought, hugging her back. Now he saw it. Megan loved as hard as her mother did. "That means a lot to me," he whispered, barely getting the words out.

As if nothing emotional had happened, Megan pulled away to return to her post at the sink. "I'm not going to call you daddy though. You can forget that shit if it crossed your mind."

"It didn't. I figured you'd just keep calling me Cal," he said to her back.

"Yeah, that works."

David's snickering over his discomfort irritated him, but he'd have to live with it today.

Shaking his head, Cal pushed open the back door and headed outside.

# CHAPTER SEVENTEEN

ANN HAD MOVED ON TO ANOTHER HOLE BEFORE SHE NOTICED THE uniformed soldier walking determinedly towards her. His eyes weren't showing much under the hat pulled so low, but she knew who he was.

And she knew who'd sent him here.

She snorted when Cal assumed a parade rest position about ten feet away.

"I left something here. I came to retrieve it," Cal said sharply, using his best no nonsense tone. He hoped it worked on Ann as well as it had on the men who'd served under him.

His hopes were dashed when she just calmly went back to digging.

"You didn't leave anything when you spent the night. I know because I checked. Why are you really here, Calvin?"

"I didn't specifically come to start an argument with you, but I will have to disagree with that statement. I left my heart here. I left it with the woman I'm in love with."

Ann laughed. "Brent pay you to tell me that? Or offer you some job guaranteed to keep you in new sports cars?"

Cal relaxed, dropping his arms and the pose. "No, he didn't

pay me. It looks like you have as poor an opinion of Dr. Colombo as I do… or rather, as I did. I don't feel like that anymore. I wish I'd listened to him. I admire his balls for tracking me down."

"Your nobility is wasted on this, Calvin. Brent only came after you because Georgia gave in and promised to go out with him."

Cal shook his head. "I don't think Dr. Colombo would have tracked me down personally if he didn't genuinely care. He could have paid someone to come in his place, but he didn't. Frankly, that man doesn't seem like the type to do anything that doesn't suit him."

Ann snorted. "All men are that type. They make up their minds and that's it. The woman they're involved with might as well step aside. She could be crying her eyes out and he would just keep on going."

"I'd always heard that same thing about vindictive women," Cal ventured closer, pacing a few steps. "I want you back, Ann. I want you to forgive me. I want another chance."

"No."

Cal swallowed hard at her flat answer, feeling genuine fear. "Couldn't you have at least spent more than two seconds thinking about it? I need a little hope here. That sounded pretty final."

"So did your poetic goodbye speech Friday night when you dumped me with no discussion of the matter. I'm not planning to listen to that kind of thing again—not tomorrow, and not five or ten years from now when you figure out I'm just some boring old lady. I think more of myself than that."

Cal paced back the other direction, but he refused to retreat. "You're not boring. You're everything but boring. A woman who drinks imported beer and belly dances will never, ever, not even when she's a hundred, be boring."

He waited for the explosion, but it never came. Laughter over his praise would have been acceptable too, but Ann just kept right on digging. Her anger was impenetrable. It reminded him of his wife's adamancy about wanting a divorce. She'd been right too, but… damn.

Had what he'd done really seemed so callous to Ann? It hadn't felt that way at the time. He'd honestly thought he'd been doing the right thing.

"The men in Mariah's folder who are waiting to date me were equally impressed by my talents. Getting a date is not my problem anymore. Trusting a man again, though? Now that's going to take a little while. Apparently sleeping with a guy doesn't mean what it used to mean. That's on me for not understanding that a sexual relationship didn't entitle me to a discussion of any sort before breaking things off. I won't make that mistake again."

"Ann…"

"Why are you here, Cal? You thought your thoughts, made up your mind, and walked the hell away. Why are you back?"

Cal hung his head. "I came to apologize… to ask you to forgive my panic. It was my ego screaming that I couldn't give you the kind of life those guys can."

"Right… and you still can't," Ann said stiffly, scooping out dirt. "Guess it must seem like they have nothing better to do with their cash than fork it over to meet women like me. Right?"

"I don't know why they do it," Cal admitted. "Guess it wasn't crazy for the ones in your folder that you dated. They met you."

Ann nodded. "Yes. They saw a video of a woman wearing six pounds of makeup and a short dress with heels. They heard her infer things about her sex life with her deceased husband that sounded appealing. They heard her admit she loved dancing. That's what they know about me. Not that I prefer beer to wine. Or that my idea of a perfect date is nachos and dancing in my kitchen, followed by great sex." She dug viciously, pushing the shovel deep. "Men see what they want to see and think what they want to think. I don't know why I'm surprised. I've always known that."

"I don't know what to say other than I'm sorry. I didn't understand our relationship. You kept going out with other men. I was living on hope."

And he hadn't understood, Cal realized. He hadn't gotten what she was doing until he saw her doing it. Now he was standing there watching her dig and he didn't really get her distress either. It felt hopeless all around.

Ann shook her head. "You know what's really strange? In the end, no matter how much money a guy spends with someone like Mariah, it's the woman they meet over a freaking toilet that actually means something. For me, it wasn't the guy with the hot balloon tour business. It was the guy fixing my pantry that I chose to sleep with because it just felt right... he felt right."

She ploughed her shovel through the dirt. "Cupid is more than stupid—he's a sadistic jerk. Mariah's just working the odds he throws in front of her. Brent's paid a fortune to meet women, but grumpy Georgia Bates is the woman he wants. Whatever she puts him through will serve him right for wasting his money."

"Look... I acted stupid because I was jealous. You're the only woman I want—the only one I've cared about in ages," Cal said firmly.

Ann grunted. "Really? Then why did you give me up so easily? You didn't even ask how I felt about you."

"I told you. I panicked. Men do that when they're scared of losing something."

"No. You gave me up because you couldn't give me time to get to the same emotional place about us. I thought dates with those two nice guys were enough experimenting for me to trust what I found with you. I certainly don't think that anymore. I'm planning to meet the other nine or ten in my match folder just to see if there's any magic to be had outside of Calvin Freaking Rodgers. Maybe I'll beat the odds. Maybe I'll find someone who makes me feel just as young and happy as you did."

"Ann... can't you cut me a damn break? I feel bad enough as it is." He started towards her, stopping only when she lifted her shovel in defense. "Now that's just mean."

"Yes. I'm mean. I'm old. And I'm too smart to let someone like you break my heart a second time. So go, Calvin Rodgers. Walk away again. You'll look very handsome doing it in your uniform.

I'm sure the people at the dance thought the same thing before I dashed into the bathroom to sob. Now go away."

Cal drew himself up tall. "No. I'm not going away. I'm not giving up. I did that and the righteousness wore off in the first hour. Stop digging those damn holes and come into the house with me so we can talk. I brought enough imported beers to get us both drunk. Maybe then we can move past this."

Now she felt violated even further. Ann gripped the shovel like a ball bat. "Who let you into my house?"

Cal swiped the hat off his head so he could glare better. "I didn't break in. Damn it, woman. Your children let me in—Megan and David. I went to see them to find out how you were."

The shovel fell from her suddenly limp fingers. "You told my children about us?"

Cal narrowed his eyes. "Yes. I did, but only the PG rated version. I'm not completely uncouth. I knew I had screwed up royally, but I was worried about you. Worry and concern was something Colombo made sure I felt before he left."

He paused for a moment, then figured he might as well spill it all.

"I told your children I loved you. The first chance I get, I'll tell your friends too. Now my father? Well, I'm going to have to ease into breaking the news to him that I hit on one of his favorite clients. It might help if we're engaged when I have to come clean. You won't want to be around when I tell him though. Dad's going to be extremely mad at me for a while."

"Calvin. How could you do that?"

The crazy fool. He'd told the world about them—well, most of it. Ann turned her back and lifted her arm. Her dirty sleeve didn't do much to stifle her new sobs. She'd forgotten how annoying and stressful and wonderful love was.

What was she going to do with Cal if she did forgive him? As if he'd heard her thoughts, Cal was suddenly there to answer the question, spinning her around and tugging her body close.

She punched his chest with both fists. "You hurt me. I fell in love with you and you walked away. It hurts to lose someone you love that much."

"I know. I'm sorry… so, so sorry. I love you too, Ann. I swear— I love you. Please be the better person and don't send me away. I promise you—I've learned my lesson."

Her arms finally came around him and Cal all but fell against her in relief. He gripped Ann's dirty chin in one hand and closed his mouth possessively over hers. How had he thought he was going to forget this? She was his perfect match in every way.

He vowed that never again would he be the cause of those salty tears running down her face. Knowing they still had a lot of talking to do, Cal finally let her ease away from his grip. He put his forehead against her dirty one.

"You have to forgive me for my moment of stupidity. I know for a fact that marriages don't work out when your wife stays mad at you all the time. And for the love of all that's holy, woman, please stop dating other men. My ego isn't strong enough to deal with thinking about you kissing those other guys."

Ann's sighing head nod said she understood his rant, but it wasn't a verbal yes or an agreement. Needing to believe they were in the process of making up though, Cal chose to believe it was a good sign whatever the nod meant.

"No, no." He gripped Ann's arms tighter when it looked like she was starting to bend over. "If you pick up that shovel and start digging again, Megan is going to turn me into her personal punching bag. I have a healthy sense of self-preservation, so I can't let you do that. Your children are both worried sick about you."

Despite sniffling back another river's worth of tears, Ann chuckled. "Can't a woman dig a few holes in her own backyard? I was just going to plant some shrubs."

"Why don't you wait until your new deck gets built? You can plant them around that. I'll help you dig next time."

Her watery gaze went to Cal's. "A deck? With a built-in barbecue?"

"Yes. David's planning the works. Dad and I will be building it.

Do not rat me out. Your children are not as civilized as my ex's new family. Something tells me they would see my betrayal of information as an ass kickable crime."

Chuckling over Cal knowing such a truth about her children, Ann rubbed her eyes with the back of her hand, until Cal grabbed it. He pulled a perfectly white handkerchief from his pocket and gently wiped her eyes and face.

"That's the best that can be done without you taking one of those mega showers that uses up a whole hot water heater's worth of water. You are seriously funky."

"It's called hard work," Ann grumbled, feeling Cal link his fingers tightly through hers.

"So you say. I'll show you my idea of hard work later—when we really make up," he said.

Her face heated just at the thought of being with him again. Luckily, the dirt hid most of it from the worried gazes of her concerned children waiting in the kitchen when they went to the house.

Both patted her face but refused to hug her until she was clean.

ANN TOWEL DRIED HER HAIR, SPRAYED IT WITH A GOOD LEAVE-IN conditioner, and then wrapped the bath sheet tighter. It literally had taken nearly an entire water heater's worth to get all the dirt and mud off. Too bad all that water hadn't washed her remaining reservations away.

She couldn't help wondering if Cal was going to hurt her again. In fact, she sort of knew he would. Wasn't that the risk of any relationship? The question was… could she handle it?

Or maybe the question was whether or not Calvin Rodgers was worth it.

She started back to the bedroom and saw Cal sitting on the side of the bed still dressed in his uniform. Hat in hand now, he stared at her when she exited the bathroom. He straightened as she came closer, but only looked at her when she sat down next to him.

"Do Megan and David know you're in my bedroom?" she asked.

Cal grinned at the question. "No. They left a bit ago. I think they wanted to give us plenty of time to talk things out. Those are two smart kids you raised. I've learned the hard way not to get between them when they're fighting."

"Their father was an intense guy, but that whole have-to-be-heard thing came from me." Ann sighed loudly, lifting a hand to her wet hair. "I've never been good at fighting... or handling the aftermath."

Cal grunted. "Me neither—said the divorced man offering his failed marriage as proof."

It should be disturbing that she found that comment funny, but Ann laughed anyway. She could tell her humor relieved Cal because he grinned and relaxed.

"When my wife left, it hurt, but it also felt inevitable. Losing you was like losing an arm. The whole time I was being stupid, I knew my life was never going to be the same without you in it. Colombo laid a well-deserved guilt trip on me, but it was your children who made me realize that in hurting you, I'd hurt both of us. I hate being this wrong, Ann. If I let you take a swing at me with that shovel, can we call it even and move on? I want you to trust me again."

"Stop," Ann ordered, snickering over his repentant tone. "I'm sure eventually Georgia would have slapped me silly and sent me after you to explain myself."

"Explain what?" Cal asked.

Ann studied her hands and then shrugged. "I needed the other guys to show me just how great you were because it had been so long since I'd had a man in my life. I knew all along that I was never going to want them the way I wanted you. And I knew I was never going to let them become anything more than a friend. The very fact that I'm still so upset about you walking away from me makes me fear you. I fear the effect loving you is going to have on my calm life more than I have words to express."

Cal offered a smile. "There's bound to be conflict at some point. We're never going to agree on everything."

Ann laughed. "Maybe not, but I'm used to getting my way. I'm also not used to letting people help me make decisions. Not even my friends." His laughter over her confession had her eyes narrowing.

"I'm a talented strategist," Cal bragged. "I've just decided that from now on we'll discuss all important matters in bed. A few high octaves ought to even the odds of me winning a few."

"Not necessarily," Ann declared.

Cal covered his mouth to keep from laughing. Her arm smack only made his amusement get louder.

"I'm being serious here, Pretty Ann. I don't want you worrying about us in the future—not ever. You're my absolute idea of a perfect match. I want to drink beer, eat nachos, and take you to bed at the end of each day. I want us to get married."

Ann sighed as she stood. She grabbed Cal's chin the way he'd grabbed hers in the yard—hard and with purpose. She looked deep into his eyes and all she saw there was desire... for her. What Cal and she had was far, far more than she'd ever hoped to have again in her life. She'd find a way to deal with the bad stuff so long as she could have all those things with him.

"Do you care what order your wishes come true? I'm really not in the mood for a beer at the moment."

"No." Cal tilted his head, eyes questioning her even while he answered.

Chuckling at his confused look, Ann turned loose of him. Guys always needed it spelled out so she unfastened her towel and let it fall to the floor.

Eyes widening over her action, Cal tossed his uniform hat like a Frisbee until it landed in a nearby chair. He grabbed both her wrists and tugged her close enough to press light kisses across her face and neck. While he was doing that, Cal made that sound...

that sound Ann hoped she drew from him for the rest of their lives.

"If we're going to get married, you need to find your balls and tell your father about us, Calvin." Then Ann pressed her mouth to his, absorbing that sound the moment it was being uttered.

Understanding at last that a love like this was worth all the risks, she happily let a still fully dressed Cal drag her completely naked body into the bed with him to finish making up.

# CHAPTER EIGHTEEN

Ann hid a smile as Cal met Georgia's glare with an innocent look. Once she told Brent what Cal was doing for him today, the man would have to consider himself paid back in kind for his good deed.

"So you're telling me that Hollywood honest-to-God and in person tracked you down and talked you into apologizing to Ann?"

"If you're talking about Dr. Colombo, then... yes, ma'am, he did. The good doctor found me *and* ordered me to get my shit together. I decided to take his advice. I do realize I'm lucky Ann's such a forgiving woman."

Georgia snorted. "Sleep lightly, Cal. She's not as forgiving as you think."

Ann walked up to Cal and leaned against his arm. "Georgia still grilling you?"

"It's worse than being reamed by a military superior," Cal replied.

Ann's snickering laugh had him slipping an arm around her.

"Food's ready," Jellica yelled.

"About time—I'm starving," Georgia said, complaining and walking off.

Cal looked into her gaze. "Why am I doing this again? I'm really not that mad at the man. One lie and he's off the hook, right?"

Ann patted his cheek. "Forget the players. Consider this as merely repaying a good deed."

"Since they're both your friends, this may end up being your wedding present," Cal declared, sliding Ann into his lap to hold her.

A shadow with fisted hands suddenly loomed over them.

"Calvin Rodgers. I wondered when I was going to get a look at you. So you're the guy who took my client from me," Mariah said.

Ann yelped when Cal put her back on her feet almost instantaneously. She stared down at her now upright body in surprise. Cal stood to full height and glared at Mariah.

"If you're out any money for Ann not dating those other guys, I'll pay her damn fees—all of them. She's mine."

"I'm what?" Ann asked in total surprise.

Mariah disintegrated into laughter. "Yes. I can see Ann is yours. Everyone can see that."

Georgia's snort broke the tension. "Stop harassing the man, Mariah. Hollywood's going to pay for me. It's all good. Nobody's going to be out any money except the hoity-toity plastic surgeon and he can well afford it."

"Mom, I was teasing him," Mariah said, her laughter dying at her mother's words. "And Brent is not hoity-toity."

Cal and Ann watched as Georgia dragged her daughter off, both of them arguing. He turned to her then. "I don't believe I'm saying this, but I'd rather deal with Megan and David than your friends."

"Too bad. They're all Stan's clients. I'm sure you'll be fixing something for each of them eventually."

"Only until my investment classes start paying off," Cal said with great relief. "I don't think I've been this excited about

# Speedy Rewards

3664 10/21/20130 9:50:04 AM 5093633

Hello Tammy

Total Points Earned This Visit:                        6
New Point Balance:                                    59
Club Status:

* Milk Pint Club: 5 more for a FREE single or Pint mi
* Frito Lay Club: 1 more for a FREE single serve bag
* Food Court Club: buy 3 more for 1,000 Bonus Points
* Good to Go Fresh Donut Club: 4 more for a FREE donut
* Krispy Kreme Club: buy 5 more for a FREE Doughnut
* Beverage Club: buy 1 more and get a FREE beverage

---

www.SpeedyRewards.com
Customer Service 1-800-643-1948
Mon-Fri 8:30am to 5:30pm EST

* This is not a sales receipt *

anything in years. I've basically been saving what Dad's been paying me. I figure that will give me my first investment money."

Ann slipped her hand in his. "I don't need your retirement to pay the bills. You can use that too."

Cal pulled her close. "We'll discuss my contributions again later... like in bed later. And we'll keep talking about my share until we come to some mutually beneficial terms. Mutual—isn't that a great word, Ann?"

"What am I going to do with you?" Ann asked.

"I swear I'm seriously going to make you a list if you keep asking that question."

Ann snickered as they walked toward the tables full of food and friends out on her new deck. With a teasing Cal at her side, she now had the perfect life.

— THE END —

# NOTE FROM THE AUTHOR

Thank you for reading *Never Say Never*!

If you enjoyed reading this book, please consider leaving a positive review or rating on the site where you purchased it. Reader reviews help my books continue to be valued by distributors/resellers and help new readers make decisions about reading them.

*You are the reason I write these stories and I sincerely appreciate you!*

*Many thanks for your support,*
*~ Donna McDonald*

**www.donnamcdonaldauthor.com**

**Join my mailing list to hear about new releases.**
**http://eepurl.com/b7-IkH**

# EXCERPT — NEVER A DULL MOMENT

## ANOTHER ROMANTIC COMEDY WITH ATTITUDE

# BOOK DESCRIPTION

*What could she possibly have in common with a man whose watch costs more than her car?*

Georgia may be slowing down a bit at sixty, but she isn't stupid yet. The idea of her genuinely dating Dr. Brentwood Colombo, aka Hollywood when he poses in her doorway… well, that's just totally insane.

Where is her dignity? Where is her pride? How did she let her snickering friends dare her into giving him a chance?

And where is the kind, caring daughter she raised? Mariah's been replaced with an evil version who keeps insisting she give the womanizing plastic surgeon who dates twenty year olds a fair chance. A fair chance at what, Georgia wonders? Breaking her heart?

No, thank you. She would rather keep her womanly dignity than see it trampled under Hollywood's expensive, polished shoes.

Now if he'd just stop talking about her perfect, perfect breasts, she might forget about him completely.

# CHAPTER ONE

HOLLYWOOD WAS TURNING OUT TO BE EVERY BIT AS MUCH TROUBLE AS Georgia had feared he would be. He'd already reduced her to begging.

"You have to help me. It's not like my phone is full of stuffed-shirt society matrons I can call. You're the only rich person I know."

Georgia bit her lip at how pathetic she sounded. Trudy sniffed at her request as she refilled her coffee mug. Was that a yes sniff or a no? She couldn't tell.

"I'm not sure how you think I can help, Georgia. I suppose we could visit my red room. I'm sure there's some things in there you might be able to use," Trudy said, shrugging at her thoughts.

Georgia stiffened on her bar stool. "Red room? Are you saying all wealthy people are into kinky sex shit these days? Okay, that's a show stopper. I'm too old to get hung up by my wrists."

Trudy barked out a laugh and spilled her coffee on the floor. "Who said anything about chaining *you* up? I'm saying you need to learn the proper etiquette for chaining a handsome plastic surgeon to the wall. Did you know that you have to use the fur lined handcuffs so you don't damage his evil moneymaking hands?"

"Are you serious?" Georgia demanded.

Trudy laughed harder and then shook her head slowly. "You have some strange ideas about wealthy men, Georgia. Have you ever considered getting professional help for that neurosis?"

"No. I raised a head shrinker from scratch. Mariah's been laying mental guilt on me since she was a teenager. When she left home, I decided I'd had enough therapy for one lifetime."

Trudy rolled her eyes. "I love you like crazy, and I guess I have no room to talk. Heaven knows, I'm no better in the attitude department when it comes to men. Not a single one has ever stayed with me more than a year or two. But don't rule out the kinky stuff. You may need to do some of it. You and I have to be damn good in bed for a man to put up with our level of shit."

"What are you talking about? I was happily married for a very long time. And I'll have you know it's taken me sixty years to hone this attitude." Georgia pushed away thoughts of Hollywood staring at her breasts before she answered the rest. "We will not be getting far enough on our bogus date to have sex. I just need to fulfill my obligation without embarrassing me or my daughter. The man is used to dating younger women and I'm in over my head. Now are you going to help me or not?"

"What do you expect from me, lady? I'm not a freaking miracle worker," Trudy declared.

Georgia lifted both hands. "I'm nearly triple the age of his typical dates, Trudy. A couple of his other wives were Mariah's age. I still don't know how I got myself into this mess, but I damn well don't want to show up looking like I feel. I need to create an image he'll believe for a night."

"What are you talking about? Are you calling yourself an old grumpy ass, granny Cinderella?"

Georgia thought about it and shrugged. "I can live with that. So will you play my fairy godmother?"

"Well, just you showing up to ask for help at all is a shock. I can see you faking a severe illness before I see you giving in to some man's emotional blackmail. Damn, you must really like him. Come on, Granny-Ella. Let's see what I can do for you."

Georgia grunted at Trudy's nickname, putting all the indignation she felt into it. "I do not like Hollywood. I promised him a date and he's going to do something amazing for Mariah's business. I'm being altruistic for my daughter's sake."

"Bullshit. You're acting all female because he's handsome and charming. You obviously like him well enough to care what he thinks. You're not doing this just for Mariah. You need to get honest with yourself," Trudy said, walking briskly away.

Georgia followed Trudy through her huge house which still managed to feel homey. Chef Trudy Baker had a lot of friends—famous friends—who liked to come for the kinds of visits family only did in Georgia's world. Entertaining semi-strangers for weeks on end wasn't something Georgia could imagine doing, but Trudy seemed to enjoy turning her home into a bed and breakfast stopover once in a while.

Trudy's house was a u-shaped, well architected ranch. She followed her down one long side until Trudy stopped in front of a closed door. Taking a big breath, Trudy let it out slowly as she pushed the door open and walked inside. She flipped on the overhead light and sighed in disgust.

Georgia stood back, afraid to go in after watching and hearing her friend's reaction. What the hell was in there? Trudy wasn't afraid of much.

"Don't hover in the freaking hallway, Granny-Ella. You wanted my damn help, so get your cranky, old ass in here."

Georgia rolled her eyes to the hallway ceiling, swore under her breath, and then braced herself. It still hadn't been enough to prepare her.

She walked into what had probably been intended to be a medium sized bedroom, but that had been converted into a giant walk-in closet. Three-tiered racks circled all the walls, and some required the tall step stool standing nearby to reach the clothes on the top tier.

In the center of the room were two enormous, back-to-back dressers, obvious storage for folded items and accessories. Installed on either side of the dressers were department store looking shoe racks with dozens of shoes on each shelf. On nearby shelves against the wall, stacks and stacks of shoes were still in their boxes and towered to the ceiling. In the bare spots where the clothing racks ended, there were also two six foot tall jewelry armoires.

"Holy shit, Trudy." Georgia's wandering gaze took in the lavish clothing with astonishment. There was every conceivable color and style. Her mind couldn't even imagine how much money had been spent to buy what was in this room. The thought of Hollywood having something close to this, filled with his watches and expensive suits, made her want to vomit. She had one black dress… well, two now after the dance she'd gone to with Ann.

"I bet I spent at least a half a million dollars on these clothes," Trudy said, looking around. "That's why I still have them. I tell myself that at least I didn't collect anything really dumb, like salt and pepper shakers, or gravy boats. Can you imagine having a room full of either of those? People would think I was crazy."

"Were all these clothes for your TV work?"

Trudy shrugged. "Some were for the show. I put getting to keep them in my contract. Then there were local appearances. Oh, and every time I was interviewed on a talk show? Well, that required a new outfit. And the schmoozing—God… the lunches, dinners, parties, not mention holiday galas. This is a decade's worth of crazy clothing purchases. I'm not a real trendy person so most of this is classy. Since you and I are nearly the same size, I'm sure we can find you something suitable for your blackmail date."

Ignoring the sarcasm, Georgia stared at Trudy's body hard. "We're not necessarily the same size. You merely borrowed a pair of yoga pants once and thought they fit you well. Spandex is very forgiving that way. I have way more boobs than you do."

"The pants did fit well and I now own four pairs. I'd wear them every day if I never had to go out of the house." Trudy snorted as she eyed Georgia's breasts. "I have just as much boob as you do. Mine just aren't as perky."

"Hey, I've worked damn hard for these perky girls," Georgia said, rubbing her forehead as she tried to ease the growing tension there. "I didn't want to borrow clothes—I just wanted some advice. I was planning to buy something new if necessary. I'm just trying not to embarrass myself... or my daughter."

"Or Brentwood Colombo wherever he decides to take you?" Trudy finished.

Georgia sighed and nodded. "Yes, damn it. Him too." She looked around the room. "Can't you just pick something for me?"

Trudy shook her head. "No. I hired a personal dresser who helped me buy and coordinate this stuff. Now I'd call Ann to come help. She has excellent taste."

"You're right. I should probably have called Ann, but she's so busy these days. Do you think she can tear herself away from Cal long enough?"

Trudy sighed and rubbed her shoulder. "They're still new to each other. We'll get our friend back in time. That initial lust happens to everyone, but it doesn't last. I've felt it many times and it always goes away."

Georgia shook her head and frowned at Trudy. The woman was the most jaded person about love that she knew—worse even than her. Even her own daughter, Mariah, hadn't been this cynical about finding herself attracted to another cop... and she'd had good reasons to be.

"Lust lasted nearly an entire marriage with me, which was a fortunate thing for my military husband who wasn't romantic by any stretch of the word. Cal's a good man and he adores Ann. Hollywood was right about that. I don't want to screw up their happy buzz by whining about my stupid date."

"I still can't believe a renowned plastic surgeon helped you chase down Calvin Rodgers for Ann. Sounds like your Hollywood is a good man too. Don't you think?"

Georgia shrugged. "I wouldn't know."

Trudy chuckled. "Well, I hope you have a lot of fun finding out. Feel free to snoop around in here and pick a few things to try on. I'll be in the kitchen if you need me. A cookbook writing friend is coming to dinner. I'm making something special for her."

Still in shock over the contents of Trudy's red room, named no doubt from the ugly wall paper peeking between the racks, Georgia looked around numbly after Trudy left her alone. Finally, she walked to the center of the room and picked up a three inch pair of red stiletto heels from a shelf. They had pointed toes and two thin straps to go around your ankle.

"Not on your life, Hollywood. Not even if you turn out to kiss as good as you look."

# CHAPTER TWO

WHO MET FOR COFFEE TO PLAN A DAMN DATE? THIS WAS SO STUPID. Didn't the man know how to send a text? They'd done that a lot when he'd been helping hunt down Cal. She didn't understand the need for this get together or why it was important to planning the real thing.

Since Trudy had obviously bought stock in black cashmere sweaters at one point in her life, Georgia had absconded with one of three identical cardigans she'd found on her scavenger hunt, as well as a surprisingly well-fitted, dark red, silk blouse that she'd worn outside her new black slacks. The new pants were slim cut, ankle length, and tapered at the bottom. The style of the pants made them look great with her favorite black ballet flats which she promised herself she didn't care about Hollywood judging as old and well-used. She'd bought the shoes at a great outlet, and in several colors, because they had looked so good on her narrow feet.

She'd topped off her mostly borrowed outfit with a dark red, jasper necklace Jellica had made for her. Jellica said the stone was worn by warriors for protection. That had sounded good to Georgia because she needed all the protection she could get from

Hollywood… or at least from her own feelings for him. The man seemed to know exactly how to push the wrong buttons. He kept her on edge and she didn't like being there—not at all.

She sighed as she walked into the café in his building, frowned as she looked around at the blandness of it, and then swore at feeling so tricked. This wasn't a café. It was damn cafeteria. She'd expected an opulence befitting his expensive gold watch, not serviceable plastic chairs and scarred Formica tabletops.

"You've got to be kidding me," Georgia said under her breath, but evidently all those standing nearby heard. Raising her chin in the air to hide her embarrassment, she tried for lofty. "I'm here to meet Dr. Colombo. Allegedly. I believe he's expecting me."

It came out sounding pompous and churlish, and being nervous wasn't helping her tone any.

"Of course. Dr. Colombo's table is this way."

"Table? Who in hell reserves a table in a cafeteria?" The woman's quick frown clued her in that she'd actually spoken the rude thought aloud. "Sorry," Georgia said. "I'm just… surprised. He has a habit of doing that to me."

Nodding, the woman patted the well-used table top. Georgia raised an eyebrow, but managed to tap down more comments. "Thank you," she made herself say instead.

"Would you like coffee or tea?" the young woman asked.

"I have to watch my caffeine these days. Water with lemon, please," Georgia answered.

A head nod later and the young woman was off. Georgia sighed under her breath and wished Ann had warned her about this place. All she'd heard about was the cozy chat and the dancing at the end of it. Hollywood's smarmy charm had probably kept her impressionable friend from noticing the worn out atmosphere.

The water soon appeared, along with a carafe for refills, and a dish of extra lemon slices. A second trip brought an assortment of finger sandwiches and petit four desserts, which she recognized primarily from being Trudy's guinea pig for her fancy baking stints. Baking had never been her thing. The only dessert she'd ever served in her house came from her local grocery store.

Georgia sipped her water, called herself crazy for being here, and worked to settle down her nerves enough to at least appear to be waiting patiently. Some forty minutes later, after she'd played two rounds of her favorite game on her phone, she promptly decided she'd been polite long enough.

Leaving the food untouched, she rose from her seat, put her unused napkin by her tiny unused plastic plate, and started across the room. An out-of-breath Hollywood nearly knocked her over as he propelled her backwards into the cafeteria. A tittering of laughter from those watching them brought out her worst reaction possible.

"What the hell do you think you're doing? Let go of me."

Hollywood had the nerve to look at her and laugh. He turned loose but didn't move away. "I'm trying to stop you from leaving. I was with a client. We ran a little over."

"You're forty minutes late. That's more than a little. The ice in my water glass melted completely while I was waiting."

"Melted ice? Is that your timer for abandoning your dates?" Brent asked.

Georgia crossed her arms, which made her breasts press against the snug shirt, because she really was a bit bigger up top than Trudy. The action of serving up her girls for his eager gaze earned her a chuckle, and a leering you're-the-only-woman-in-the-world smile that would have made any female of any age forgive the bastard.

"Since I don't do dates outside of those I get blackmailed into, I can't properly answer that question. You're the only dating expert here."

"I'm not the expert you think I am," Brent insisted.

He reached out a hand and put it on her arm. It felt really good to her, so Georgia stepped away. His bad behavior would not be rewarded with her total capitulation. Partial maybe… but not total.

No way, Jose. She was not buying his charming bad boy routine ever again.

"Please, Georgia. Stay at least for coffee. I still have an hour before my next appointment. I'm sorry I kept you waiting so long."

Glancing around, she saw concerned glares directed her way. She wondered what kind of female riot a total brush-off would cause. What the fresh hell was this shit? Did Hollywood have every woman in existence under his spell?

"Maybe I'm the only woman in the world who would chastise your bad manners, but I don't give a rat's ass. Didn't you think of sending me a text to let me know you were detained?"

Her retort had him taking a step back. Hollywood thought about it for a moment and then shrugged. "I guess I didn't think of it… but you're right. I could have taken the time and let you know what I was doing."

And just what was she supposed to say to that straight-up admission? Georgia hadn't expected a mostly sincere apology. Damn it. Couldn't he just consistently be the ass she thought he was? It would make this so much easier.

"Fine," Georgia said tightly. She turned and trudged back to the table, ignoring the whispering sighs of relief going on. Her eyesight might be going as she got older, but nothing was wrong with her hearing.

A fresh glass of ice water appeared before Hollywood even had the chance to get seated. Her begrudging thank you drew a wicked smile from the woman serving it. A cup of coffee and a cream pitcher was put in front of her very late date. Hollywood said nothing as he fixed it the way he wanted. She watched, her gaze mesmerized by his elegant fingers stirring the cream into the fragrant black liquid.

Brent lifted the cup and took a sip. "Hello, Georgia," he said softly, lowering the cup to the table.

"Hello, Hollywood," Georgia said back automatically.

"You look very nice today. Red looks as great on you as blue does. Your choice of hair color is very flattering with all those shades of gray and silver. You've put together quite the package for me. I'm honored you took the time."

Tempted to lie that she hadn't gone to any trouble at all, Georgia squirmed in her chair to keep from fibbing. "I prefer to let God choose. He's the ultimate stylist."

Georgia was grateful when Hollywood chuckled at her comment. Usually only her closest friends laughed at such irreverent snark. He could have easily seen it as a subtle dig at his godlike profession, and she was suddenly glad he hadn't. Why was she always the worst version of herself with this man?

"Okay, I confess. Mariah's responsible for the haircut and the highlights which account for at least three of the shades. I had to hold the woman back from the ten or twelve she'd planned on giving me. I've truly no desire to look like every other painted blonde."

"You don't," Brent said. "Far from it. You look... perfect. That's the only word I can think of that fits."

His sincere sounding statement had her swallowing hard, especially when accompanied by his encompassing look of pleasure as his gaze roamed her face and hair. She didn't find her voice again until his gaze dropped to her chest and then fled quickly. Much more of that sort of nonsense and her face would match her shirt.

"Does that sort of stuff get you laid as often as I keep thinking it probably does?"

Brent grinned as he lowered his cup. He grabbed a sandwich from the tray. "Wow, I am really late. The bread is already stale. These usually hold up a little better."

"You're spoiled," Georgia accused, noticing he had deftly avoided answering her original question. She had no choice but accept his redirect as a big, fat yes.

To her utter surprise though, Brent nodded at her spoiled accusation.

"I am. Spoiled... and bored with females in general." His gaze came to her as he finished the sandwich. "Except when I'm with you. Then I come alive. It's the strangest damn thing."

Georgia laughed at the wonder in his voice. She wasn't even sure why. Maybe it was flattering. Or maybe it was just hilariously ironic. "God, you need serious help," she told him.

Her heart beat hard against her ribs when he smiled and laughed. His self-effacing nod was her undoing. "Damn you, Hollywood. I don't want to like you."

"Welcome to my world... except I've moved on in my thinking. I've gone from liking you to considering how on earth I'm going to convince you to get naked with me."

"Stop that," Georgia ordered, glaring without the anger she should have been feeling over his admission. For damn sure, her pulse should not be racing with excitement. "That is never happening."

"Good thing I'm an optimist," he said.

She watched him suspiciously as he lifted a petit four. "Do you like chocolate?" he asked, holding it where she could inspect it.

When Georgia nodded politely, he set the delicate pastry on her plate. He chose another and put a strawberry one on his plate before looking at her again.

"Chef Trudy Baker makes these for me. I did some work on a friend of hers. It was pro bono, but Chef Baker insists on paying me with food. I can't refuse her offerings. I get a personal delivery every month. They freeze well. The woman's a magician in the kitchen."

"Trudy? She's also a tight-lipped, tight-ass hussy," Georgia fumed. "Trudy never said anything about knowing you personally. I'm wearing her clothes today and she never said shit about knowing you when I borrowed them. How do you know her? Did you date her too?"

Her comment earned her a masculine snort. She had no idea what it meant, other than it didn't seem to be any sort of admission. She was starting to read him fairly well.

"No. I didn't date her, Ms. Paranoid. She's friends, or used to be friends, with one of my ex-wives. Chef Trudy Baker is a great woman."

Georgia lifted both hands in the air. "Then why in hell aren't you sitting across the table from her instead of me? She's... she's..." Georgia searched for the nicest words she could think of to set him straight. "Trudy's way more your type."

The dessert paused for a full three seconds on its way to sliding between his perfect white teeth. Eventually Hollywood chewed, but the whole damn time he was staring at her. She didn't like it when he looked at her that way... or at least she didn't want to like it.

"We had no chemistry," he finally said. "I never had it with any of the women I married after Henna's mother. I wasn't aware of that until after I met you. Like I said... you make me feel alive."

"Chemistry?" She spat the word at him.

Brent laughed at her frown, leaned over, and picked up the dessert on her plate. He lifted it to her mouth.

"Eat," he ordered gruffly. "Maybe the sweetness of this little cake will help with the sting of my honesty and your friend's betrayal. I have no excuse, but imagine Chef Trudy Baker keeping our illicit friendship from you. The nerve of her."

"Stop making fun of me," Georgia ordered, smelling the tempting chocolate. It was worse because she knew exactly how good it would taste.

When Hollywood waved it under her nose over and over, she finally leaned forward and took a tiny nibble. He laughed at her action, so she swallowed and leaned again to take the rest into her a mouth all at once. His fingers scraped against her teeth and she drew sharply away at his shiver.

Sensual awareness ran through her instantly, too strong to deny as she held his sexually interested gaze. Bemused by her own reaction, she watched as the man across from her swallowed hard and put his now unsteady hand back on his coffee cup.

Her mental debate with herself over their attraction was not going well. Her conscience was shaking her head at her body's denials and laughing hysterically.

"It's a good thing I don't have do any surgery this afternoon," Brent finally said, breaking the spell.

Georgia put her hand over her mouth as she chewed. There were a thousand retorts she wanted to make about what had just happened, but not a one was possible with a mouth full of Trudy's delicious cake. Damn it. The woman was supposed to be *her* friend, not Hollywood's.

And Hollywood was supposed to a be a jerk. Well, he was in some ways, but he was so much more too. It was the *more* that made her nervous. Just like now, when he was leaning back in his chair and staring at her.

"What we have is what I meant by chemistry. It's been missing from all my relationships until you. I desperately want in your pants, Georgia Bates. It's been a long damn time since I've felt that way about a woman. So here's your out. If you aren't equally willing to see where our physical chemistry takes us, then consider our date... called off."

Georgia picked up her water and drank, giving herself time before she tried to speak. This was the best possible outcome of this farcical coffee date. Wasn't it? Hollywood was giving her an honest out. All she had to do was pretend to be unaffected by him.

She set down her glass harder than she'd intended. Probably not a good way to show she was calm. "What about Mariah?" she asked.

Brent shrugged. "I guess she'll lose a client until I need a companion for some event again. I'll still spread the good word about her business, if that's what you're asking."

"My daughter is hard to fool. If you quit getting dates from her, she'll know I'm the damn reason," Georgia complained.

"Woman, I'm giving you an *out*," Brent declared, waving a hand dismissively. "Isn't that what you want? To not go out with me?"

"No," Georgia declared back. "I mean, *yes*... but... *no*. I want things to be like they were before you decided we had chemistry."

Hollywood stared at her for long moments and then burst out laughing. It went on so long it made her squirm in her seat again. His glare wasn't mean when he got control of his mirth. No, it was determined... scarily determined. That worried her more... and made her stomach flutter like it had the first time she'd laid eyes on him.

"Sorry to disappoint you, Georgia. That's not how chemistry works. I want you. Obviously, only you. You're the name I call out in the shower these days."

"No!" Georgia denied. "No, I'm not."

Brent leaned across the table. "Yes. Yes, you are."

"I'm sixty-two," Georgia hissed, leaning over the table. "Men don't feel that way about women my age."

"Well, you don't know everything then. I feel that way about you... and you can't control that. So... tough shit," he said, sounding pleased he'd come up with a swearing answer.

Georgia leaned back in her seat, stunned further when he rose to leave. Hollywood got several steps away from the table before she finally found her voice.

"Wait... Hollywood, wait," she said quickly, needing to stop him. Why though? Why did her chest hurt at the idea that she might have truly offended him?

Georgia stood too, and walked to stand in front of him. "Keep your out. I don't need it. I'm not afraid to date you."

"Really?"

She blew out a breath and glared. "Alright, I'm lying. Of course I'm scared to death of this crap, but I'll be damned if I let that be the reason we call off a simple date. I made a promise and I intend to keep it. So when do you want to do *this*..." Georgia waved her ringless hand in front of him."... *thing* you want to do."

"Are you talking about our date? Or me getting into your pants? The answer to the second question is *now*. I want to do that now."

Her hand smacked his chest without thinking about it. "I'm talking about the stupid date," she hissed between clenched teeth.

His disbelieving laughter travelled over her, getting caught by every nerve ending she possessed. Before she could process how weak it made her knees, Hollywood's lips were brushing across hers with the sure precision of a man who'd been planning every nuance of it.

Then he turned and simply walked away from her.

"I'll text you the details... about our *date*," he said wryly, calling the statement out over his shoulder.

Georgia stood there watching him leave with every female's startled gaze locked onto her. Hollywood had kissed her—God, nearly frenched her—right in front of all the damn cafeteria workers.

"If I live to be a hundred, I will never understand that man," she protested, touching her mouth.

It was the loud and very satisfied giggling of those watching her that sent Georgia back to her seat to retrieve her purse. Once again, Hollywood had played her for a fool and gotten his way.

# CHAPTER THREE

"How was coffee?"

"Fine."

"How did Brent treat you?"

"Fine."

"So when's the big *date* happening?" Mariah asked. She dropped a healthy amount of whole wheat pasta onto her mother's plate before covering it with fragrant sauce. John's catering service was amazing. She was eating well these days.

Georgia looked around the nice kitchen. "This place is wonderful, Mariah. Where's John this evening?"

"Working late," Mariah said quickly, not wanting to share more. Undercover only worked if it was kept a real secret. John was going to be gone at least four days. She was getting used to his occasional disappearances, but she still missed him when he was gone.

Georgia looked down at the food her daughter had set in front of her. "Smells great."

Her lack of enthusiasm must have shown more than she thought because Mariah frowned. "What's wrong? Did I give you too big a portion?" Mariah asked.

"No… and don't look at me in that assessing shrink sort of way. I really don't know when we're going out. Hollywood said he would text me the details, but he hasn't been in touch yet."

"Text you?" Mariah sat with her own plate. "That doesn't sound like Brent. He usually has it all figured out. He's a contingency planner and very particular. I've often wondered if he was a bit OCD."

Georgia sighed and picked up her fork. "I'm like that too… usually… but that doesn't seem the case with our situation. I don't even know what day or which week. I guess Hollywood has to clear his social calendar first. I refuse to worry about it. I'll hear from him when I hear from him. I'll worry about it then."

Mariah ate in silence for a few beats. "What's wrong, Mom? You know you don't have to do this. A date is supposed to make you happy and light-hearted, not drive you crazy. Let me tell Brent you've changed your mind about going out with him. You're not my client. You're my mother. He'll have to understand.

Georgia snorted. "No. This is Hollywood we're talking about. He always makes me crazy." She ate, chewed, swallowed… and then sighed. "I think I make him crazy too. That doesn't make me feel better though. It just complicates things."

Mariah put an arm on the table and leaned her face against her fist. "The people who bring the most change into our lives always seem to be the ones that make us most uncomfortable."

Georgia laughed. "Thank you for the analysis, Dr. Bates. And here I thought I was only getting spaghetti for dinner."

Mariah chuckled. "I'm your child, Georgia, which means I'm impervious to your snark. Does Brent have you so rattled that you feel the need to get defensive with your friends too? Or is it just me?"

Georgia groaned in frustration and forced herself to take a bite before answering. "What friends? Turns out Trudy knows Hollywood personally and she never said a damn word. I had to hear it from him."

Mariah shrugged. "Smart woman. I imagine that kept you from

grilling her for hours. I'd have done the same thing in her case if I didn't want to color your impression of Brent."

Georgia thought about it and decided that was fair. Trudy protected people's reputations with carefully worded explanations. Not for a moment did she believe Trudy would have given Hollywood any dirt on her either.

Her sigh was one of concession. "You're probably right about the reason Trudy stayed quiet, but it was embarrassing as hell to hear about their long time friendship while I was wearing her clothes and eating her damn petit fours."

Her daughter's giggle set her mouth quirking. "Okay. I suppose I can see the humor too. But I can't wait until you fix Trudy up with somebody hideous. I hope the men you find for her do something really horrible for a living."

"Like what?" Mariah asked.

Georgia chewed and thought. She lifted her fork. "Hot dog vendor—like at the ball games. Or popcorn. She'd hate falling for a man who was so focused on one food... and especially if it was nothing healthy at all."

Mariah chuckled around a mouthful. She shook her head. "No entrepreneurs with food businesses in my database. How about an accountant?"

Georgia shook her head. "No, no. Save the account for Jellica. God knows that woman can use the practical help. All her new age woo-woo doesn't get her far. She needs a damn keeper."

Mariah nodded. "Okay. I can see that. Opposites do attract and I have an accountant who's not typical. Greg would probably like Jellica's body. He's big on fitness. She's keeps herself in great shape for a mother of two teenagers."

"It's all that yoga. Got to say all my older friends like to keep in shape. Exercise and taking care of yourself is not really optional after a certain age if you want to keep living a full life," Georgia explained.

Mariah nodded. "Guess I should have gotten salads for us, huh?"

"I eat enough salad," Georgia said firmly. "But I don't have pasta as much as I used to. This is delicious."

For a few minutes, they stopped talking and just ate in the comfortable silence that comes with being with family. Georgia didn't have company for dinner every night though, so she enjoyed the conversation... and hearing Mariah talk so excitedly about her business.

"So how did things work out with that boy who wanted to date older women? Did you ever find him the perfect date?"

"Boy?" Mariah asked.

"The tattooed one Della likes," Georgia said, pointing at her arm.

Mariah's brow wrinkled because she hadn't heard from him a while. "You're talking about Elliston. Mom, he's in his thirties. He's not exactly a boy."

"He's half my age. I ask only because I caught Della giving him the interested eye one day."

"The interested eye?" Mariah giggled.

"She was looking at his ass and sighing. That's what I call *interested*, especially at her age. Those hormones of hers are probably screaming his name."

Mariah's laughter filled her kitchen. "That's the way you look at Brent when he's not looking that way at you. Are your hormones screaming Brent's name?"

"Yes. They're yelling 'run' but I can't seem to do it. Hollywood is spoiled, Mariah. He thinks everything revolves around his cute ass which every woman he comes into contact with wants a piece of. That man does not need any encouragement. He does not need me as part of his harem."

Mariah smiled. "Brent's very attractive and very successful. That's a powerful combination. But if those traits had brought him real love, he'd be married and happy, and not using my services. Instead, Brent's been divorced multiple times and has been dating just to get companions for an evening—and I don't mean the really fun kind. I'm talking dance partners, like he did with Ann. Since you're both my mother, and a client so long as you intend to go out with him, I can tell you this one other thing about him. One of the biggest complaints I have about Brent is that he's an outrageous flirt who doesn't sleep around. The man talks a good game, but he doesn't put out."

Georgia snorted. "Now I know we're not talking about the same man. Hollywood told me bluntly that he wants in my pants."

Mariah's laughter rang out and she found it hard to stop. *"Brent did not say that to you,"* she said between laughing breaths.

*"Verbatim,"* Georgia insisted, finishing her pasta. "But I knew better than to take it seriously. I think the women who work at the cafeteria in his building are placing bets on it happening though. They giggled when he kissed me and giggled harder when I ran the hell out of there."

"Brent kissed you in public—like in front of people?"

"Yes, Dr. Bates. I didn't take that action seriously either. I mean, look who we're talking about here. The man's lips have no doubt travelled far and wide. He was quite proficient at kissing."

"Mom," Mariah said, choking on her laughter. "Brent's not like that. He doesn't kiss reluctant women. He does not get demonstrative in public. He's… reticent."

"Oh my darling naïve daughter," Georgia sang as she carried her plate to the sink. She rinsed and added it to the dishwasher, which looked newly installed. "All men are like exactly like that. The best looking ones are talented at hiding it from women they aren't lusting for. And Hollywood is hell and far from being an exception to anything. He's one of the most lusty males I've ever run across."

～

HENNA NEARLY WALKED BY THE STUDY, BUT THE CHINK CHINK OF ICE cubes against glass had her stopping. She peered inside the big room. There was a fire in the hearth, but no lamps lit.

"Dad? Are you in here?" she called out, looking around in the dimness.

"Yes. I'm here," Brent said, not wanting his daughter to think he was hiding.

Henna walked to a table in the far corner and turned on a lamp. It helped a little, but wasn't bright and glaring.

"Why are you drinking in the dark? Even better... why are you drinking at all? You haven't done that in ages. I could smell the bourbon out in the hallway."

"I am drinking because I want one night where I don't lie awake thinking about being with her. She's turned me into a damn teenage boy. It's not fun being a man in this condition, Henna."

Henna was glad he wasn't talking about her mother for once, and yet not really happy about her father moving on emotionally with the unhealthy object of his current obsession. Determined to be supportive though, Henna slid into the adjacent chair and turned to her parent.

"Good luck with the drinking thing. It didn't work for me. The memories are just finally starting to go away on their own."

Sighing, Brent slid his glass onto the table beside him. "I'm setting another poor example for you."

Henna shrugged. "I'm nearly thirty, Dad. I think I can handle my father having an emotional crisis or two."

"You're twenty-seven. That's not 'nearly thirty'. That's practically a baby still. And I'm supposed to act like an adult at my age. I'll be fifty-five in May and that's chronologically accurate."

Henna snickered at her father's protest. "Well, I'm old enough to own my own screw-ups. I chose to marry a man with a known history of cheating. What happened to me was my own fault. At least you married fairly nice women after Mom died. They just had bad children who were royally pains in both our asses."

Brent sighed. "I tried to keep them from hurting you, Henna. I know I failed at that too. I know you married to escape the house and the selfish people I kept bringing into it."

"That might be a little true," Henna said, grinning when her father's handsome face turned sadly her way. "Okay, maybe a lot true. But I could have picked a better man to escape with. I'm not stupid and it wasn't like I was in love with him. I knew I wasn't. I was just naïve about relationships, and desperate to feel loved, which I will never be again. I've definitely moved on from that phase."

"Well, I'm in real love," Brent said sadly. "But I don't recommend it. Hurts like hell."

Henna giggled. "Is that the bourbon talking?"

"Three sips in? Hardly." Brent sighed and raised an eyebrow. "A whole bottle wouldn't help me get over her. You know what the worse thing is? Georgia hates me. She hates my career, the way I talk... pretty much everything about me. She's attracted, but not about to give in to her feelings. Why am I even bothering with her?"

Henna laughed at the miserable expression on her father's face. Reaching over, she pushed the bourbon closer to him. "Now I know for sure we're talking about the sassy bitch at the dance— Georgia whatshername. Here, finish this. That woman requires alcohol to discuss."

His grin over her teasing had Henna grinning in return.

"Please Henna, watch your language. Give me the illusion that I raised you better. I need it tonight."

"She says far worse things, Dad. You know that's true."

Brent nodded. "Yes, but I want my daughter to be a better person. Georgia's covering up hurt with her speech... I can tell. Her swearing helps her feel tough enough to deal with life."

Henna held her father's gaze. "I understand that you want me to *sound* like a better person than her. But I can assure you that I'm already a genuinely better person. I take after my father... or so I've been told. And Georgia isn't being a bad person either. When I met her, she was just crudely defending her friend who I may have slightly insulted because I was mad at myself for letting you down."

Silence filled the room after her statement, until her father lifted his glass and rattled the ice cubes again.

"You never let me down, Henna. I shouldn't expect you to attend things like that dance with me. I should have enough friendships with women that I could have asked a friend to go. But I don't have those sorts of casual relationships with women. I never have. I tend to become a caveman when I like a female, but frankly, I like that about myself."

"Well, there's no arguing with a caveman, now is there? Are you really in love with the Georgia woman?" Henna asked.

Brent looked at his daughter and nodded. "Yes, at least I'm fairly sure I am. This time is not like the others, Henna. I'm well aware the woman has the power to make me just as miserable as she could ever make me happy. Every day with her might be a fight, but I still want to be with her. Georgia doesn't put up with any bullshit. She doesn't kiss my ass to get her way. She's..."

"Brutally honest and genuinely attracted to you for you, instead just being after your money like the others were?"

"Yes," Brent whispered, grateful his daughter got it.

"In theory, I agree she sounds like the perfect woman, Dad. But she'll definitely drive you crazy. She's got a bad attitude and I don't think she respects you like she should."

Brent's laughter was a surprise to both of them. He heard his daughter laughing too. "Instead of earning her respect, I tricked her into going out on a date with me. I tricked her and now I'm afraid to call her. She's only going to give me one chance and I know one date will never be enough to fix her opinion of me. So I'm putting it off. She's turned me into an emotional coward."

"Whoa... that's a very harsh conclusion." Henna snickered at her father's fear, lifted a hand to stifle her amusement, but finally let the laughter escape as it needed to.

"Do you think my trickery is funny? Or the fact that now I'm afraid to face what I've done?" Brent asked his child.

"I'm laughing at my own wicked thoughts," Henna replied.

"You should ask Georgia to come to the gala on Saturday. Make all her worst fears about you come true."

"No," Brent said firmly. "They'll all be here. I can't do that to her. Hell, I shouldn't be doing it to me. I don't know why they keep coming every year, but they tell me they feel like they should be included in the "Colombo family" sponsorship. I never know how to turn them down. It seems so rude to deny anyone's support for charity."

"Duh, Dad… your ex-wives have their own club and that club has one agenda. Those three women are coming to be sure there's no chance of you every reconciling with any of them."

"There's absolutely no chance of that ever happening," Brent said firmly. "I'm far smarter than that, and there's also the fact that Georgia Bates has wiped other women from my mind. What I have with her has reminded about what love is supposed to feel like."

"Wow, I'm starting to think you are crazy. Listen to me, Dad," Henna said firmly, leaning over to put a hand on his arm. "If you host the gala with someone like Georgia as your date for the evening, the exes will run screaming from the place and take all my step-whatevers with them. Georgia's older, bolder, and if they say anything nasty, she'll go for their jugular. The entertainment value alone could be priceless. I'll even stay for the whole evening if you invite her."

"Georgia is not a pit bull for hire, Henna. Those negative reactions are just her self-preservation kicking in. Mariah said her father was in the military. I'm sure Georgia hasn't had an easy life."

"She's more like a pit bull than you realize, Dad. I know because I tangled with her and got bit," Henna insisted, thinking of their altercation, and how Georgia had verbally defended her friend. "Bet Georgia could chase away those French poodle women you married without having to do more than growl in their direction. They're already going to be appalled to know they've been replaced by someone like her. Her sass will just seal your madness in their minds."

"One comment about her age from them would doubly ensure Georgia will never speak to me again. She doesn't have any idea how youthful she is as a person. I can't take that risk, Henna. Would I like to have Georgia by my side Saturday? Yes. But that doesn't make thrusting her into the middle of my poor marital history right."

"Did you really think you were going to get to keep that opinionated woman under any circumstances? Georgia's got a terrible attitude about men—worse than mine even. Find someone nicer to fall in love with."

Henna paused to let the bad news resonate. She hated her father's sad nod, but she would hate more to see him hurt worse than he had been by loving the wrong people. They'd both done enough of that. She rubbed his arm again.

"Invite her. I think Georgia would enjoy the conflict and end up helping you because of it. Maybe you two will end up friends after. Who knows? Maybe you can do her facelift one day, like you did for the French poodles."

"I wouldn't touch a single thing on Georgia's body with anything other than my hands. She's sincerely beautiful to me as she is, Henna. I mean that. Don't harbor the wrong idea of my preferences just because of what I did for a living. I did your mother's surgeries for her sake, not for mine."

Henna patted her father's hand. "I know, Dad. Mom said that too. So no facelift for Georgia. But think about what I'm suggesting. If Georgia somehow did survive the gala, who knows? Maybe that would prove she was the right one. Any woman that didn't run screaming after seeing the exes would have earned a real chance with you. I'd welcome her with open arms myself... maybe."

Though he knew his daughter meant her last comment as a joke, he couldn't see Georgia surviving Saturday as well as Henna did. Brent looked away and nodded as he stared at the fire. He and Georgia barely knew each other. Would one nice, quiet date change her resistance to him? Doubtful. Henna was at least right about that being mostly hopeless.

When he turned back to see if his daughter was really being serious about inviting Georgia to the gala, Henna was already gone.

# CHAPTER FOUR

TERRIFIED AT THE AMOUNT OF SWEARING AND MUMBLING ANN WAS doing, Georgia watched her normally calm friend dig through the racks, pulling outfit after outfit out to view only to return it moments later. All she could be grateful for was that it was happening in Trudy's red room instead of some pricey clothing store where snooty salespeople would be glaring at her over it.

Trudy wandered into the room and laughed at Ann standing on the ladder. "What's she looking for?"

"I have no idea," Georgia said, being gut honest. "But I'm getting more scared by the minute." She turned and glared at Trudy. "The only reason I'm still speaking to you is that Ann insisted you'd have something better to wear than anything I could afford to buy. You didn't tell me you knew him."

Trudy snickered. "I wasn't ready to get into it the other day. Now I am. So where is Brent taking you for your infamous date?"

"His house," Georgia said, shrugging. "I'm to be his date for some gala something or the other he hosts every year. Guess he's afraid to be alone with me."

Trudy stared open-mouthed. "Are you shitting me?"

Her reaction made Georgia laugh. "No. Why?"

Trudy turned away and swore a few times before ranting. "That son of a bitch. I thought he was a nicer guy than that. I can't believe this."

Georgia rolled her eyes. "Ann's clothes hunt was already striking terror in me. What do you know about my date that I don't? It sounded pretty public and safe when he suggested it."

Trudy looked ready to scream as she pushed back her hair. "God... men. I hate them sometimes. Climb down, Ann." She turned to Georgia. "The Colombo family throws that event— meaning all the people who still claim to be Colombos too. His freaking ex-wives will be there. You're being set up, Georgia. You can't go to that event. No telling what kind of hell his former wives will put you through."

Georgia stood staring at an angry Trudy for what seemed like hours to her. The information wasn't computing in her brain. Why would Hollywood do that to her when he trying to get into her pants? Or had that been some sort of game he was playing?

Ann put a hand on her arm, gently bringing her attention back to the room. Georgia blinked as she looked down into Ann's worried gaze. She glanced at a still agitated Trudy. "I don't get it. Why would he do that me?" she asked both her friends.

Ann rubbed her arm harder, glared at Trudy while she did it, and then rolled her eyes when Trudy didn't explain. "Brent's obviously trying to get even with you for your... *you know*... your bad attitude whenever you talk to him."

Trudy nodded. "Probably true, but that's not the whole answer. I just never wanted to believe Patricia's stories about him. She said Brent's used to getting his way in the relationship. She told me she never had the upper hand, not once during their marriage. Since Patricia is a master manipulator, and equally used to getting her way, that would be saying a lot for her to admit something like that."

"Why should I care what a jilted woman says?" Georgia asked.

Trudy shrugged. "She also told me Brent's still not over his first wife, which I imagine is true as well. Talk to Mariah if you want a professional opinion. All I can say is Brent's obviously got some real issues. I'm sorry to be the one to point out all the potential bad stuff behind his offer."

Stunned, Georgia held out a hand to stop Trudy' speech and walked away. She stared at the red room wall paper, letting it all sink in. Had Hollywood been faking his interest? Had he been setting her up this whole time? Her chest hurt at the thought and she rubbed the space between her breasts—the same breasts Hollywood couldn't seem to stop himself from staring at every chance he got.

Foolish. She'd been foolish to even indulge in the fantasy of them together and grateful now that she hadn't yet given more voice to it. Her foolishness was going to bite her on the proverbial ass Saturday, just like she'd been fairly sure was going to happen eventually.

At her age, she certainly should have known better. Whatever Hollywood had been trying to prove by his faux courtship, his success at making her feel like an idiot was assured. But it wasn't just her own consequences that she had to face.

If she didn't go through with the date now, what would Dr. Brentwood Colombo, asshole date extraordinaire, do to Mariah? Or her business? That worry was alarming too.

Pride aside, she couldn't let things play out in a bad way. She couldn't let her daughter suffer for her foolishness. Georgia hung her head, sighed, and then turned back to her friends.

"I'm going Saturday, even if it's all completely true. I have to go. If Hollywood's that much of a lowlife, he likely wouldn't think twice about quietly putting out something negative about Mariah's business. I can't take that chance. I have to go there and deal. If he gives me shit after Saturday, I'll give him the worst rating Mariah's database has ever seen. He'll never get another decent date out of her once I expose him for the creep he is. I'm sure there's worse things I could do to his reputation once I'm at the place where I can think things through."

"Georgia... you don't want to put yourself through this," Ann insisted. She looked imploringly at Trudy, then back at Georgia. "We know you like Brent. We just pretended to go along with your protests because we knew you were scared. Now you could get really hurt here. He's not worth that."

Georgia drew herself up tall. She hadn't survived this long by letting *anyone* make her feel like less of a person. She had no plans to start with Brentwood *The Bastard* Colombo.

"What I liked about Hollywood was the idea that I might have been wrong about him. It would have been a nice surprise and I admit I harbored a fantasy or two. But I'm not as naïve as his daughter. I'm a survivor, no matter the crisis, and that's something no one is going to take from me. I will survive this too." She looked around the room and lifted her hand in a circle. "So find me the best armor you can. I'm going to need it to face Hollywood's former harem."

Trudy stopped Ann from heading back. "No. I know what Georgia needs. She needs a lip zipping display of undeniable wealth." She walked to a rack and pulled out a cream suit with gold studs on the jacket sleeves and skirt. "Closest thing I have to real armor. The gold studs are real gold. This suit is worth over a hundred thousand dollars. Everyone there will see it and know the gold is real. They won't be able to say any denigrating shit about off-the-rack anything."

Ann ran a hand over the finely made suit, and looked at Georgia. "You're going to need a bright blouse, some heavy gold jewelry, and a gold rinse to turn those silver strands of yours the right shade. We'll go back to Mariah's person. You also need to get a professional manicure and makeup to match the blouse we pick."

Georgia nodded and forced a tired smile. "I trust you both. You know I wouldn't be able to do this without your help."

Trudy reached out, took both of Georgia's shoulders in her hands. "You don't have to do this at all. Screw Brent and his exes. I care about you more than I do about any of them, and that includes my shallow friend who married him. Now you may have given Brent some grief in the short time you've known him, but you at least sincerely liked the man for himself. You aren't using him financially so he doesn't deserve the chance to hurt you. And you don't need to deal with the sick kind of comparison shit that could happen. Not everyone with wealth is petty, but it only takes one or two to hurt your confidence."

"If this was just about me, I wouldn't go," Georgia said softly. "But this is about Mariah. I can't let him hurt her. I won't. Let him have his revenge if that's what this is about. It's one evening of my life, but I'll have what I need to protect my daughter's business afterwards. Then I'll never have to see the bastard again."

Trudy nodded, still looking unhappy. "Okay. I have everything you need but the sass. You're going to have to find that inner bitch yourself. Take buckets of attitude with you."

"Oh, you know me," Georgia replied, gently pushing Trudy's hands away. "I have enough sass to fill up your red room twice over. Now I have to go retreat and lick my wounds. I hate it when I make a mistake this big. But I'll be back tomorrow to pick up my armor. I'd never go to war without it."

"God… Georgia. Brent does a lot of these charity things. He raises a lot of money for good causes. I can't imagine why he'd intentionally do this to you. He never struck me as a malicious person. Mostly, I felt sorry for him," Trudy exclaimed.

Georgia hugged Trudy. "Don't worry. Thanks for warning me. It would have been horrible to walk into that situation and be blindsided. Now I won't be and that's the best I could hope for in the circumstances. I will not let Hollywood reduce me to being pathetic over this. I swear I won't."

She turned to Ann. "Thanks for helping me. I'll do everything you say needs done to look my best. Just make the hair stuff temporary, so I can go back to being my normal self next week. I don't want any reminders of my craziness."

"Done. Just temporary rinses, I promise," Ann said fiercely.

Georgia nodded. "Good. I'll see you all later."

She didn't have to swipe any tears away until she got to her car.

The floodgates opened then and refused to be stopped. She studied her haggard face in the rearview mirror.

"Sixty-two and a fool for a womanizer. What did you think would happen with a man who looked like him, Georgia?"

It was a misty-eyed drive home, but Georgia got there in one piece.

The quiet of her once again empty nest bothered her today, but that was just her feeling sorry for herself. She was glad Mariah had found a new life and a good man to love her. Every woman deserved to have someone in their life like John.

"Maybe I should get a dog," Georgia said, thinking out loud.

If she did, she'd get a female dog—a fellow bitch. They'd grow old and be sassy together.

Yes, definitely a female dog.

The last thing she needed in her life was another male of any species.

**www.donnamcdonaldauthor.com**

# OTHER BOOKS BY THIS AUTHOR

**The Perfect Date Series**
Never Is A Very Long Time
Never Say Never
Never A Dull Moment

**Never Too Late Series**
Dating A Cougar
Dating Dr. Notorious
Dating A Saint
Dating A Metro Man
Dating A Silver Fox
Dating A Cougar II
Dating A Pro

**Art Of Love Series**
Carved In Stone
Created In Fire
Captured In Ink
Commissioned In White
Covered In Paint

### Non-Series Books
The Wrong Todd
SEALed For Life
A Secret Dare
Saving Santa
Mistletoe Madness
No ELFing Way

**Visit Donna's website** to see more books.

# ABOUT THE AUTHOR

## DONNA MCDONALD

After 35 years of doing everything for a living except writing books, Donna McDonald published her first romance novel in March of 2011. Forty plus novels later, she admits to living her own happily ever after as a full time author.

Her work spans several genres, such as contemporary romance, paranormal, and science fiction. Humor is the most common element across all her writing. Addicted to making readers laugh, she includes a good dose of romantic comedy in every book.

*How To Contact Donna...*
www.donnamcdonaldauthor.com
email@donnamcdonaldauthor.com

67108534R00114

Made in the USA
Lexington, KY
02 September 2017